CHRISTMAS WRAITH

Haunted Everly After
BOOK TEN

REGINA WELLING
ERIN LYNN

Christmas Wraith

ISBN- 978-1-953044-36-5

Cover design by: L. Vryhof

Interior design by: L. Vryhof

http://reginawelling.com

http://erinlynnwrites.com

First Edition

Printed in the U.S.A.

Contents

Chapter 1

A thousand bees buzzed in my ears. A curtain of darkness snuffed out the light.

Hours or seconds passed. Time had no meaning, and what did time matter anyway? Davina had been inside me when she crossed over, and something had gone very, very wrong. She'd killed me. Or worse.

Was there something worse? I wasn't sure.

And where was the light? Wasn't I supposed to go into the light when I died?

I drifted through endless night until a sound penetrated the darkness.

"Hello, my darling girl."

I recognized a voice I never expected to hear again.

"Grammie Dupree? Am I dead?"

"Not exactly." My grandmother chuckled.

"What do you mean not exactly? I'm asking you a yes or no question. Am I dead or alive?"

"What do you think?"

I'd have sighed if I could still feel my body. Not being able to set my mind racing. "I think if you're here, I must be dead or dying. Did you come to help me cross over?"

"Not exactly." In life, Grammie Dupree never used

1

two words when she could fit in ten, so these brief answers were out of character. Or maybe not. Maybe people changed when they died and went into the light. I guessed I'd probably find out soon enough. Except, now that I thought of it, there was a hint of stronger emotion in her tone.

"What, then?" Panic suggested the faint scent of brimstone. "Am I not welcome on the other side? I've helped a lot of ghosts find their way there. Seems like that should buy me a ticket through the veil, and I'm not a bad person."

The comfort of her presence surrounded me like a hug. "Of course, you're not a bad person, but this wasn't supposed to happen. I came back because what's happened to you is all my fault, but I didn't mean for anything bad to happen. It's not your time. You have to go back."

"Happy to." I still couldn't see her or anything else, but the darkness felt less like a weight on my soul now. "Tell me how."

She hesitated so long I wondered if she'd gone.

"Are you there? What's the deal with my body?" I explained that the last thing I remembered was helping Davina hug her long-lost son right before she'd crossed over and dragged me into purgatory or wherever this was. My body could be on the inn's kitchen floor or in the morgue, or anywhere in between, depending on how much time had passed. "Davina's gone, right? I remember her telling me it was time, then there was screaming. I'm a little hazy on the details after that."

"She's gone, but there's a trial coming," came the cryptic reply, followed by, "Forgive me, love, but it's time to wake up." Grammie Dupree snapped her fingers, and I did. Sort of.

My eyes popped open. I was still in the inn's kitchen, but not on the floor. Several feet away, Jason still stood right where he'd been, with his arms around his mother. Well, technically, his arms were around my body where his mother had just been, but she wasn't there anymore, which was, I supposed, the good news of the day.

"Thank you." Jason hugged me hard. "You have no idea the gift you've given me. I feel like I've been reborn."

I heard myself say something soothing and saw myself pat him on the back. It took me a moment or two to realize I was watching all of this happen from the outside. Another moment passed before the implications set in, and still, one more before I realized who was in my body.

My father always said I had his mother's eyes. This was taking that to the next level.

Stunned, I watched while my grandmother assured Jason it had been her pleasure to help and made excuses to leave. Without my having to prompt her, she asked him to keep quiet about what we'd just done for him. "People would talk. People in this town always talk. It might not be good for either of us if they do."

"Your secret's safe with me," Jason agreed, and we left him standing over his pastry table with a sad smile on his face but also with peace in his soul.

Outside, after a somewhat shaky walk across the lobby, Grammie Dupree closed the door behind her and leaned back against it for a few seconds to get her bearings.

"That was….interesting," she deadpanned, then pulled herself together and opened my purse. "I need a hanky."

"There's a napkin in my coat pocket," I answered helpfully. She hesitated briefly, then closed the purse and tested both pockets before pulling out the napkin to blow her nose. Had she heard me tell her where to look? I couldn't be certain. She didn't say anything to me as she walked down the steps, but I noticed her hands shaking as I followed her to the car, where Drew waited.

I hadn't had nearly enough time to process my new reality, so I wasn't thinking straight when I reached for the door handle and lost my balance when my hand went right through. Time slowed to a snail's pace as my face passed through the door, then the seat, and I wondered if I might fall all the way through the car, the entire earth, and keep right on going. Maybe I was just the worst ghost to ever live. Or die. Or not die, or whatever it was I had done.

To my great surprise, I did not fall through the earth because my thoughts distracted me long enough for my subconscious to impose itself on my altered reality. I ended up on my hands and knees with my head sticking out through the floorboard.

"If you're quite finished flinging yourself around, get in, and we'll chat with your young man. Unless you think we shouldn't tell him. I could pretend to be you."

"You can see me, then. That's comforting, I guess. No, we're not keeping secrets from Drew. Just tell him what happened." The sooner, the better, because I wanted to hear the rest of the story, too.

The key to interacting with the regular world was to forget I wasn't part of it. My second attempt to get in the

4

car ended with me in a near approximation of a seated position. Close enough, anyway.

"Everything go okay?" Drew leaned in for a kiss and was surprised when Grammie Dupree held up a hand to stop him.

"Not exactly," she said. He settled back but kept his body angled toward hers. Mine. This was really weird. She echoed my thoughts. "There's a story to tell, and it's a dilly. You'd better prepare yourself, young man."

Drew cocked an eyebrow at the term. "Young man?"

In a gesture I remembered from childhood, she waggled a pointed finger at him. My memory superimposed the shape of her fingers over mine. "Take me home. Please."

Now both of Drew's eyebrows shot up. "Are you okay? Did you bump your head or something?" He leaned closer to inspect, but she pushed him away. His voice carried a slight echo, but hers didn't. Again, weird day.

"Or something," she agreed. "This may be hard to believe, but there was a slight mishap, and now we have a dilemma on our hands." She pronounced it die-lemma. Freudian slip?

Since Drew hadn't cared whether or not Davina put an end to my ghost-seeing ability, he kept his face carefully blank while trying to gauge my current mood. "The door? It's still open?"

I wanted to hear the answer as much as he did.

Grammie swiveled in her seat to look me in the eye as she answered. "I'm sorry. I didn't mean to cause such a fuss."

"You call this a fuss?" I fired up. "It's not a fuss. A

fuss is something minor. This is not minor. This is major. It's the ghostly grandmother version of Freaky Friday, and I want my body back." I had never spoken to my grandmother with such disrespect and half-regretted it immediately. But only half.

"Who are you talking to?" Drew wanted to know, but his gaze passed right over me when he looked into the back seat. "I left you alone for half an hour. Even you can't have run across another body that quickly."

"That was harsh," I muttered. But fair. Grammie Dupree found the comment amusing.

"No. That would have been easier. We should probably have this conversation when you're sitting down."

"I am sitting down," Drew quirked a smile, but it didn't reach his eyes. Even the most patient man in the world has his limits.

"Not here. Take us home."

"Okay." Drew dropped the shifter into reverse and hit the gas, leaving me sitting in midair while he backed out from under me. So far, in my opinion, things on this side of the veil sucked.

"Stop." I heard her yell, then saw the car rock a little as he jammed on the brakes. "Pull forward again."

"Why?"

"Just do it. I'll explain later."

Drew whacking the car into drive and pulling back in beneath me didn't improve my mood, nor did the peal of her laughter at my expense.

"I fail to see the humor in this situation," I sat scowling while Drew simply stared at her.

"Sorry. It's okay. You can go now." To me, she said,

"Stop thinking so much. Just let things happen naturally."

I'll give her credit for attempting to contain her mirth. She was about as successful as the Arch Deluxe served with a glass of New Coke, but she tried, and she was my beloved grandmother, so I let it go. In the process of deciding to be the better ghost, I realized the car was moving, and so was I.

One problem down. A million or two to go. Did I mention how weird it was to see my body doing things I had no control over? Still, with the strange turns my life had taken since my divorce, I thought I was bearing the strain pretty well. Go me.

"That's home." I pointed and accidentally poked my hand through the seat. "I bought Catherine Willowby's house when I moved back to town."

"You think I don't know that? Been watching over you since the day you were born, wasn't stopping just because I died."

The knowledge warmed my heart. Or the blank space where my heart used to be.

"Know what? Watching who? You're not making sense." Drew pulled into the driveway and dropped the shifter into *park*.

Unable to help myself, I reached for him, then flinched when he shivered.

"Inside," Grammie's mirth had subsided. "I'll tell you everything."

Chapter 2

The living world looks different from the non-living side. It wavers as if being viewed through something nearly transparent but not quite, like a curtain of water. I supposed, once I thought about it, the curtain effect was probably what the ghosts meant when they used the word *veil*.

Excuse me if I'd been expecting some gauzy or lacy number, like from a wedding gown or something. Language is a funny thing.

When she heard my voice, my dog came running down the hall. Molly danced toward me, then stopped and dropped to her haunches, her head tilting to the side as she looked at my body and then at me. Molly could see me, which didn't come as a surprise. I wasn't the first spirit she'd encountered since she'd come to live with me.

"Who's this, now?" Grammie was a dog lover. Always had been. She bent to hold a hand out to Molly.

"Molly." Drew and I spoke at the same time.

"She's a good girl," I said.

"I can see that for myself." Tentatively, Molly got close enough to have her ears scratched while her eyes stayed locked on me.

"It's okay, sweet girl. I'll be back to myself in no time." I knew the words probably meant nothing to her, but I hoped she found my tone reassuring.

Having heard half the conversation did nothing to ease Drew's mood. "There, we're inside." His body blocked my—our—progress as he shed his coat and hung it over the newel post. "Talk."

I wanted to throw myself into the safety of his arms but didn't because the mental image of me passing right through him was more than a little off-putting.

"He's pretty comfortable with the woo-woo stuff, but this isn't the same, so if you could—"

Grammie Dupree shot me a quelling look. "It's best to rip off the bandage, I think." She turned to him and held out her—my—hand. "Sadie Dupree. Nice to meet you."

Drew took a step back. "I can't tell if you're trying to be funny or what."

"There's nothing funny about any of this," I said, but he didn't hear me. Naturally.

"Or what." Grammie Dupree confirmed. "Definitely *or what*." She took off my coat and tossed it on top of his. "Everly's right here with us, and she's fine. For the moment, anyway. Be polite and offer an old woman a cup of tea, would you? I'm parched, and there's a lot to tell."

"Okay," Drew led the way back to the kitchen, but I could tell he wasn't okay by the set of his broad shoulders and the way he kept glancing back at her. We'd been together long enough for him to have seen some strange stuff, and he'd accepted the weirdness with an aplomb most people couldn't pull off, but everyone had their limits, and I worried we'd reached his.

"Black tea," Grammie Dupree said. "Good and strong, mind you. None of that herbal or green nonsense for me."

If he hadn't known something was up before, Drew would have picked up on the difference between my and my grandmother's tea preferences. I was an herbal girl, all the way. He set the pot of water on to heat, got out a cup and saucer, and filled a tea ball with loose-leaf pekoe but said nothing until he'd poured hot water into her cup and settled in the seat across the table. I noticed he didn't get out a cup of his own.

"Talk," he ordered. "And don't leave anything out."

"That Lucille Bennett shouldn't have meddled with things she didn't fully understand, and Leandra Wade isn't any better. Half-witted fools, the pair of them." She blew on her tea to cool it, then indulged herself by draining half the cup at one go and closing her eyes in bliss.

"If I stipulate there was meddling by women who should have known better, will you kindly get on with the story?" Drew leaned forward to pin her with a look. "I want to know what's happening to Everly."

"Keep your shirt on, young fellow. I'm getting to it."

I'd lived with Drew for a few months, trained with him in the gym, and seen him deal with my crazy life in a way that made me feel seen and supported. Now, his jaw clenched so hard I felt the phantom pain, and his eyes flashed with fury. Controlled fury, but even so.

"Not fast enough," I grumbled and got a dirty look for my trouble, but she softened and spoke directly to me.

"Mrs. Partridge was a ghost."

You could have knocked me over with a feather...or

wafted me away with one. Whichever worked best.

"Who?" Not having been part of my distant history, Drew was in the dark.

I shook my head. It wasn't possible. Mrs. Partridge couldn't have been a ghost. I remembered her vividly.

"Geraldine Partridge and her husband lived next door to my son. Ginny was a lovely woman who passed just before Everly's third birthday."

"No. That can't be right. I remember coming home after the first day of kindergarten and seeing Mrs. Partridge on her porch." I shook my head harder. "She asked how I liked school, so I told her all about meeting Jacy and how my teacher was really nice. Then, I showed her my coloring pages and how I hadn't gone outside the lines. She smiled and told me I was a good girl."

"I watched Everly after school." For Drew's benefit, my grandmother repeated enough of what I'd said to give him the gist of my relationship with our dead neighbor. "Two years after Ginny's death, Everly came home full of the story of her first day at school. When she told me what the nice Mrs. Partridge said about her coloring, I did what I had to do. I couldn't have Kitty getting after the girl on account of her gift, could I? It was my duty as her grandmother to protect her."

"What did you do?" Drew and I spoke at the same time and with equal dismay.

I remembered my grandmother's mutinous expression quite well, as I'd seen it on her face every time she locked horns with my mother, which was a common occurrence in my childhood. Seeing it on my own face both jarred and brought back memories. Good ones and bad.

"I realize now I might have dilled Everly's pickle, but I thought it was the right thing at the time."

Rather than trying to unravel the pickle metaphor, Drew repeated the question. "What did you do?"

"How much has Everly told you about her grandfather?"

"Just that he died before she was born."

By all accounts, my grandfather had been a man of many interests blessed with a short attention span that he indulged by becoming capable at a number of pursuits. A fancy way of saying he could turn his hand to just about anything, and his CV included a varied list of wildly disparate jobs, including a two-year stint as a traveling hypnotist on the state fair circuit.

"You have got to be kidding me." As soon as she mentioned my grandfather, I knew where this was going. "He taught you hypnosis, didn't he? And you used it on me to keep me from seeing ghosts."

"He taught me how to hypnotize people," she repeated for Drew's benefit.

And that is what she had done. Behind my parent's backs, no less. Then again, she'd caught on to my ability before my mother had. Or had she? Whenever I got my body back, I'd have to ask.

"I loved my daughter-in-law," Grammie told Drew. "Very much. I still do, but we didn't see eye-to-eye when it came to spiritual matters. I was afraid she wouldn't accept Everly's ability, so I thought it best to turn it off until Everly was older and she and Kitty could come to terms."

"And your method for interfering was to hypnotize

12

Everly against her will?" Drew's voice gets really quiet when he's annoyed.

Grammie Dupree goes the opposite way. "She was five years old," she nearly shouted. "Kids that age don't know what their will is or should be. That's why God made adults. I figured if I could hold things off long enough, Kitty would come around to my way of thinking, but I died and crossed into the light before she did."

"Without telling me anything."

She acknowledged the oversight with a nod but didn't address my concerns.

"I did a right fine job of it if I say so myself. Then, along comes Leandra Wade and her half-cocked hoodoo, and what does she do? Drills a stupid hole right through the block I put up. The next thing you know—"

Drew finished her sentence, "Ghosts realize they can haunt Everly, and she can't do anything to stop what happened to her." Condemnation dripped from every word.

Nodding, my grandmother rose, lifted the kettle to ensure it had enough water, and lit the burner for a second cup of tea.

"Which brings us up to today and Lucy's meddling." As Grammie busied herself with the tea, Drew pressed fingertips to the center of his forehead as if to ease the onset of a headache. I wanted to help with the pain, touch him, and tell him I was here and relatively okay, but I couldn't do any of that.

"Are we getting to the part where you're in Everly's body? Because that's the part I'd really like to hear. Is she in there with you? You said she was okay, but I don't see how I can trust you after everything you've done."

"Don't get huffy with me, young man. You may be a damned sight better than that idiot she married, but Everly's my blood, and I'm not letting anything happen to her. You want to know the whole story, and I'm getting to it, just need to wet my whistle. You got any cookies? It's been a while since I had a cookie."

Drew blinked slowly, shook his head, got up, and fetched the cookie jar. He plunked it down in the middle of the table. "Go nuts." His patience might be long, but it wasn't endless, and his tone was the harshest I'd ever heard him use.

"You're scaring him," I kept my voice even and respectful. "Please, Grammie, He needs to hear that everything will work out." So did I, in case she was wondering.

She gave me a look that I recognized as shame. "I meant well. Things didn't turn out the way I planned, and once I'd crossed over, I saw the damage I'd already caused, so when Lucy announced her intention to meddle, I knew I'd get my chance to come through and fix my mistake."

A tear formed in the corner of her eye. My eye. Someone's eye. Seeing it, Drew sighed and put on his placating face. "I'm sure Everly appreciates the intention."

Did I?

Learning about my mother's psychic abilities had brought us closer than we'd ever been. Her approval of my relationship with Drew didn't hurt, either, but my bad marriage and her dislike of my ex hadn't been our only issues. While I could have done without the actual haunting part of being haunted, and I certainly didn't like that people had died, the experience brought positive changes into my life. And those people would have been dead with or without being able to haunt me.

I'm Everly Dupree. I help the dead find peace whether I want to or not. That is the story of my life and, maybe now, the story of my death, but I certainly hoped not.

"Just tell me what happened when Davina tried to close the door." He must have felt my desire to touch her and offer comfort because Drew patted the hand lying next to her cup and saucer. This was a weird situation.

"That was the first problem, right there." Grammie dunked her cookie in her tea. "There never was any door to close. I don't know where Lucy got that foolish idea in the first place. Probably from Leandra."

Had Momma Wade mentioned a door? Or was it Kat Canton, the psychic medium from Oakville, or Davina herself? I couldn't remember.

"Then, what was it? A wall?"

"You've heard of the veil between worlds?"

He nodded and circled one hand to indicate she should get on with it.

"The veil is not some curtain strung on a line between this world and the next. The veil is a living thing attached to each of us when we are born. Think of it like a coat of mirrored glass. The kind you can only see through in one direction. When you die, your spirit passes through the veil to reach the afterlife. It's generally a one-way trip, though some pass through before their time and get sent back. Others, like me, find their way back when the need is great enough."

His forehead wrinkling, Drew said, "Sounds like Harry Potter's cloak of invisibility."

"I don't know who this Harry Potter is," Grammie waggled her hand back and forth. "But if you want to call the veil a cloak, that's fine, and you can wipe that pinched look off your face. Most people cross over into the light when they die. The ones that stay between the light and the veil become ghosts. Ghosts generally have their own problems and better things to do than watch you all the livelong day."

When he only offered her a bland look, she explained. "Because it's a one-way street, people like you don't see spirits unless they want you to. People like Everly see more, but not many are so strong they can't tell the living from the dead. I blame myself for passing along such a powerful psychic talent."

"And you thought you could fix the problem by the power of hypnotic suggestion?"

She shrugged. "Seems I did. For a time, anyway. All I wanted was to give her a chance to be like everyone else, and that was the only way I knew to help her shore up the weak spots so she wouldn't have to deal with the spirit side of things until she was ready."

"Weak spots?"

She acknowledged the question with a nod and continued explaining. "You know there's more than one way to communicate with those on the other side. Clairvoyants are seers; they see into the world of spirit, and clairaudients hear the voices of those in spirit. You got your touchers—like Lucy Bennett—who read items."

"Kinetics." Drew clarified. "Psychometry."

Grammie nodded. "If you like fancy terms. Then there are the feelers who tune into emotions, and so on."

"Yes, I get all of that. Are you saying that people who experience psychic phenomena more viscerally were born with weak spots in the barrier between them and the next world?"

"Keep your shirt on. I'm telling this my way. But yes, your darts are hitting the bullseye. If someone's born with a weak spot over the eyes, they tend to be clairvoyant. Over the ears, we're talking clairaudient. Hands make a toucher, heart you get a feeler. The thinner the barrier, the clearer the connection to the other side. Make sense?"

It did to me, and Drew's no fool. "Sure. Everly was born with weak spots in her veil. You gave her a posthypnotic suggestion to strengthen those spots. That lasted until Leandra made a hole over what she called Everly's third eye."

"Some call it the seat of intuition and perception. Others call it the portal to the soul. Once opened, it never closes." She nodded as if that said it all, but it took Drew a minute to work through the implications.

"You're saying that because Leandra fooled around in that particular spot, Everly can't close her eyes or ears to the ghosts that haunt her. I can't imagine what would happen if I couldn't tune out things I don't want to hear."

"He does do that," I said. "Telling him to hang up wet towels is like telling the wind not to blow."

"That's a man thing." She wasn't talking to him, but he didn't know that and brushed the stray comment aside.

"Leandra took away Everly's choice. It's as simple as that."

"You ain't so dumb, young fellow," Grammie Dupree crowed her approval.

"I'm smart enough to know that you can call it a veil, or a barrier, or a damn invisibility cloak, but that's just semantics," Drew pinned her with a look. "And I'm smart enough to see you took Everly's choice away just the same as Leandra."

A short silence ensued. "I suppose I did. That first time, anyway. Today, I came to give it back and to fix what Leandra and Lucy screwed up. My intentions were good, but we all know which road is paved with those things, and it didn't go quite like I planned."

Finally, we'd come to the part I wanted to hear.

"I suppose I could have warned Lucy what I meant to do before I grabbed onto her. She held on, but I wasn't letting her do any more damage to my girl, so I hauled her skinny ass out of there and shoved her into the light."

"That would explain the screaming, but not...all of this." I pointed from me to her.

"I'm getting to that," she said, closing her eyes to bring back the scene in her mind. "I knew I had to stop Lucy from going through this stupid door business. I guess I didn't account for the rebound effect or that she'd be dumb enough to keep hold of Everly when she should have let go. When she finally did, Everly went one way, and I went the other. We ended up like this."

Drew rose to pace between the table and the stove. "You keep talking to empty space, so I assume Everly is not in there with you."

18

"I'm here, and I'm okay," I said, but couldn't muster up the energy to make him hear me. "Tell him."

Her face flushed with embarrassment or shame. I hoped it was both because the longer she spoke, the more annoying the story became. "She's here and wants me to tell you she's fine."

"Davina was only doing what Everly wanted," Drew said. "You could have respected her wishes."

"That's the trouble with people these days. You think wanting something's a good enough reason to have it, whether it's good for you or not. Lucy fiddling with things wouldn't have stopped Everly from seeing spirits. Leandra's dirty finger put paid to that."

"Then why did you interfere at all?" I couldn't hold the question back. "If Davina's door wouldn't change anything."

She looked at me. "I didn't say it wouldn't change anything. I said it wouldn't stop you from seeing spirits."

Drew glanced at the space where I was, then back at her.

"It doesn't matter, anyway. What's done is done. I got to Everly in time to drag Lucy out of there before she did any more damage."

"Any more damage? You don't call this damage?" I gestured to my spiritual form.

"During the scuffle," she sighed and finally gave Drew what he needed to hear. "Lucy hauled Everly into the afterlife but only part way."

"Only?" Drew went pale and sputtered. "You mean she's a ghost."

Seeing his face, she rushed to reassure. "I told you,

she's here. With us. Not dead. More like disembodied."

"As if there's a difference," Drew said, glaring at my grandmother. "And for what? For nothing, that's what." Where his face had been white, it now turned red.

"No. Drew. Don't say it," I shouted. I'd have had to drop the bomb on my grandmother at some point, but I preferred to be the one punching the launch button.

"It would behoove you to watch your tone with me," Grammie put on her stern look, which had a lot less impact on my face than it would have if it had been her own.

"Hmpf." Drew huffed. "It would have behooved you to get more facts before you fooled around in Everly's head. It might surprise you to know that she didn't get her psychic ability from you. She got it from her mother."

Grammie's mouth fell open as she slowly began to shake her head. "That can't be true. I'd have sensed it in her."

Drew jammed the point home. "I guess you're not as powerful or as smart as you thought." He rose. "I'm taking Molly for a walk." Hearing the magic word, Molly followed him out, but not without one last look at me first.

Chapter 3

The sun had already set on my first day as a ghost when my grandmother and I stood in the middle of my bedroom. Feeling like my whole world had been turned upside down, I watched Drew toss his clothes into a box. He'd returned from his walk in a calmer frame of mind.

Had it been just this morning when I'd awakened in my own bed, in my own body? And now, here I was, watching my boyfriend make space for my grandmother to sleep in our bed while I couldn't even talk to him. Welcome to my new life as the ghost of Everly Dupree.

Somewhere under the layers of bravado I'd put on for my grandmother's sake lived the desire to spend an hour sniveling in the fetal position under the bed.

"I'm sorry," Grammie said, moving around to sit gingerly on the opposite side of the bed. She'd followed me in there and didn't think to ask if Drew minded. He didn't seem like he did.

"Nothing to be sorry for." Drew tossed a black tee toward the box, grabbed it when it snagged on the edge, and refolded it before adding it to the stack. "You didn't mean any harm, and this wasn't your fault. It was a series of choices that resulted in the current situation. Blaming yourself doesn't solve anything. It's what you do about your choices that counts."

I wondered what it had cost him to put his anger back in the box.

"Aren't you just a spreader of wisdom?" Cocking her head, she gave him a steady look. "Or maybe of something smelly that makes your garden grow."

Drew paused in the middle of packing, thought for a moment, and burst out laughing. "You're probably right on both counts. Everly's told me a lot about you."

Grammie laughed. "Is that a good thing or a bad thing?"

"A good thing." He leveled a steady look back at her. "Because the way she's talked, she doesn't harbor a single doubt that you love her. I can see that for myself. And because you love her, I know you won't rest until she's back in her body."

"You got that right." Brows fiercely beetled, she rose to pace the room. "Soon as my head stops spinning, I'll figure something out."

"Could it be as simple as you going back where you came from?" Drew cut her off. "Wouldn't Everly just slide right back into her body if you slid out of it?"

Her hand stopped its restless plucking at the comforter and rose to palm her face. "Maybe it is that simple." She wore my face, so when I tell you she looked like her fire had gone out, I know what I'm talking about. My face had looked exactly the same when my marriage imploded, so it wasn't difficult to recognize. "Get on over here, Everly. We'll give it a go."

"Are you sure? It could wait until tomorrow. You look like you could use a good night's sleep, and it's not like I'm going anywhere."

"What did Everly say?"

"Hush, now." She waved off any further questions and rose to spin slowly in place, her eyes going unfocused as she searched for something only she could see. She stopped once, peered at the wall on my side of the bed for several moments, then completed a second rotation.

"It's no good," she finally slumped back on the bed, propped her elbows on her knees, and dropped her head into her cupped hands. "I can't bring the light, and if I can't bring the light, I can't go into the light."

"I knew it probably wouldn't work," Drew sighed. "But it was worth a try."

"Don't worry. We'll figure something else out." I clamped down on uncertainty. She didn't need to deal with my doubts and worries on top of her own. "We're Dupree women, right?"

"Nothing keeps a Dupree woman down."

Heartened, I agreed. "Not cheating ex-husbands with more golf clubs than brains, not skanky former friends with no morals, not seeing ghosts when you didn't expect them. Nothing."

It was difficult to imagine that the woman sitting before me was actually my grandmother when all I could see was my face, but I tried because it didn't do us any good if I couldn't get past the shock of it all. I'd always wanted to be just like her when I grew up. Our current situation took that notion to another level…one that existed in the weird zone.

Her personality was the same as in life: a little salty, but underneath the sharp was plenty of sweetness. In that respect, I guess we were opposites because I tended to keep the sharp side of my tongue to myself unless provoked.

"That's the truth." Having heard only her side of the conversation, Drew agreed with her. "And you're two Dupree women working together to solve a problem. My money's on you."

"You're a nice young man," Grammie rose and patted him on the cheek. "If we're counting blessings, I'll add the chance of getting to know you to the list. Tomorrow, you'll tell me all about yourself and your family."

"Anything you want to know. Is there anything I can do to make you more comfortable now? Maybe a snack or a glass of water."

Her fire coming back, she waved him off. "I know where the kitchen is. I can feed myself if I get peckish. I did enjoy watching television of an evening. I don't suppose Dancing with the Stars is still on."

Drew shrugged. "I couldn't say, but we'll check." He dropped the last items of clothing in the box and went to the bathroom for his razor and other toiletries. On his way to the living room, he detoured to the front stairs and set the box on the bottom one.

Grammie goggled at the size of the flat screen hanging on the wall but settled dutifully into my reclining chair and flipped up the footrest. "Bring on the ballroom."

But she frowned when Drew hit the power, and the screen lit up. "What are all those little squares? Where's the TV Guide?" Her hands searched for the booklet she'd always kept tucked into the side of her chair at home. "How am I supposed to find what's on?"

"I guess TV has changed some since your time. We use a lot of different streaming apps now."

"Streaming apps?" Her forehead wrinkled. "You'd better show me because I don't have a clue what an app is, much less what a river has to do with anything."

Drew's forehead wrinkled to match hers while he tried to figure out what she meant. When he connected the word streaming to her mention of a river, he explained as well as he could. Finally, he took the remote, and set up a profile for her, adding shows from the list she gave him, then helped her through the process of choosing one.

"If you change your mind about snacks, I'm sure we have microwave popcorn, or there's an air popper in the kitchen. I'd be happy to show you how to work it."

Grammie's brows shot up, and she grinned. "I didn't die in the dark ages, boy. I know how to nuke a bag of popcorn."

"Sorry." Drew's face went dull red. "I didn't mean to insult you."

"Don't worry; you didn't, so you can tell your face it doesn't have to look like someone kicked the dog. You go on along now and unpack your pitiful box. I'll watch something and head off to bed soon. It's getting late."

Drew looked at his watch. Twenty minutes past eight. This had been the longest day of my life, and I couldn't help thinking he probably felt the same.

"I think I'll just take a book upstairs, and I have work in the morning. Will you be okay here alone for the day?"

"I won't be alone. Everly's here."

Whatever his thoughts, Drew kept them off his face. "I'll just lock up, then, and let you get some rest. Goodnight, Sadie. If you need anything, just holler."

As Drew made his way up the stairs, I stayed behind in the living room with Grammie. It was strange, sitting here with her like this. It was almost like having her back, but not quite.

But I didn't want to dwell on that right now. I just wanted to spend some time with my grandmother, even if it was in this strange new form.

We watched TV for a little while, Grammie critiquing the dancers on Dancing with the Stars and me nodding along. It was nice to have this moment of normalcy, even if it was just for a little while. But eventually, Grammie started to get tired, and I could see her eyes drooping.

"You've had a long day. Why don't you get some sleep? I'll...well, I don't know what I'll do. Probably hang out and practice saying boo."

When she headed off to bed, though, I went upstairs to check on Drew.

He'd unpacked his things in the largest of the spare rooms upstairs, the one nearest the bathroom. Away from my grandmother and finally alone, he sat on the side of the bed, his shoulders bowed from the tension.

"I'm so sorry." He couldn't hear me, but I couldn't help myself. "I didn't know this would happen, and now, you're stuck in just about the weirdest situation I can possibly imagine. Maybe you should run now. I wouldn't blame you." Without thinking, I reached over, put my hand on his knee, and then snatched it back when he shivered.

"Everly? Is that you?"

I touched him again to prove it was and saw him relax a little. Plus, he didn't flinch from the sensation this

26

time, which spoke volumes about his character.

"Is it weird that I feel better knowing you're here?"

He got two taps this time.

"Two taps for no?"

When I tapped once, he nodded. "I got it. Crude but effective. I'll keep it to yes or no questions. I know Sadie said you were okay, but are you?"

One tap and he relaxed even more.

"I love you."

One tap on the knee, another on the hand. He got the message and smiled.

Chapter 4

"Just tap the button with the little speech cloud." Hovering next to my grandmother, I pointed toward the icon, and winced when she rapidly stabbed at the screen, managing to open several random apps.

"Stop! Touch the square button. No. The square button. That's the round one."

"This is stupid," she grumbled. "In my day, you picked up the phone, put your finger in the dial, and twirled if you wanted to talk to someone. There was no tapping."

"Did I say tap? I meant touch. Once. Gently," I said. "And there were push-button phones in your day."

Finally, she got the text app open and, after a few false starts, navigated to Patrea's text thread. I felt like I'd run a marathon. With one foot tied behind my back.

"Okay." I worked at keeping my voice calm while I pointed to the text input box. "Next, you need to touch right here." We both got a chill when her finger intersected with mine. "Touch. It's not a real button; you don't have to jab it. You know what…let's just try a voice text, hmm? See the microphone? Touch it."

"Fine." She did and then ranted about technology while her words scrolled onto the screen.

If I'd had the ability, I would have taken a few cleansing breaths. As it was, I walked her through clearing the rant and got her to touch the microphone again.

"Just say this: can you meet me at the shop? It's important," I said, then winced when she all but yelled at the phone. In the end, the text went out, and within a minute, Patrea's affirmative reply hit my inbox.

"It will take her a little while to get there. Gives us enough time to walk over."

"You want to walk; go right ahead. I'll be driving that overgrown station wagon of yours."

I may have whined. I'm not proud of that.

"I'm not sure your license is still valid."

She already had the keys out of my purse, and there wasn't a thing I could do to stop her.

"I guess it's a good thing everyone will think I'm you, isn't it?"

Resigned, I followed her out the door and bit my tongue when she spun the tires while backing up.

"She's got some snot to her," Grammie said.

When Grammie Dupree stopped in the middle of my street, I tried to grip the door handle, which didn't work anyway and earned me a quelling look.

"What's dual climate control supposed to mean?" Apparently, we weren't moving forward until she'd adjusted the heater and fiddled with the radio to find a station that played something she liked. She could have done all of that while we were still in the driveway, but what would be the fun in that?

"It means I can control the temperature on my side of the car in case I want to be cooler or warmer than you do." Everly thought about it for a second. "You know, if I had a body and could touch the controls."

She gave me a sideways look with one eyebrow cocked as if my explanation sounded ridiculous, and probably, to her, it did. Comparatively speaking, my grandmother hadn't been dead all that long, but long enough there were automotive options that didn't exist while she'd been alive.

I wasn't sure what to say and ended up not saying anything at all because my cell phone rang through the Bluetooth connection and made her jump a little.

"What's that?" We were still blocking the street.

"Pull back in the driveway. Jacy's calling."

"From the radio station?"

By the time I'd explained how the system worked, Jacy had hung up, which was probably for the best. The news about my current situation was better delivered in person. Seconds later, a text message scrolled across the screen.

—*Are you okay? Answer your phone.*

"She's worried about me." But since we were headed to the shop anyway, I didn't even try to explain to my grandmother how to send a voice text over the car's system. It just wasn't worth the time or effort. "Are you sure you want to drive? It's only a half-mile or so. Not that far to walk."

"You expect an old lady to walk half a mile on snowy sidewalks? What if I fall? What if I break a hip?"

It occurred to me that my concerns should have had less to do with her driving my car than with her driving my body.

"Age is only a state of mind." My tongue might have

been firmly lodged in my cheek, but she didn't seem to find the comment amusing. "And in this case, it's a literal state of mind. You're not in the body of an elderly woman anymore. But it's fine if you want to drive. It's just that I haven't had this car all that long, so I'd appreciate it if you exercised a little caution."

I might as well have waved a red flag before a bull. Muttering dire imprecations under her breath, my grandmother dropped the shifter into drive and rocketed away from the house like it was the zombie apocalypse, and her brains were listed on the menu as the delicacy of the day.

Still in a seated position, hovering in midair, I watched her get almost to the end of the street before I felt a mighty tug in the area of my stomach, and looked down to see a thin line, like a strand of light arching from my astral body to my real one. I had about a second to find the sight interesting before the tether rubber-banded and yanked me toward the car.

Once she noticed the lack of my presence, Grammie threw the shifter in reverse and came back for me. I saw the flash of backup lights heading my way but had too much momentum going to stop. I shot right past her and out the front of the car.

"Quit fooling around," she said when we finally got ourselves aligned again. Nothing ever goes easy.

"That used to be the furniture store." Grammie pointed to a flat-fronted, two-story building at the end of the block. When I looked at where she pointed, the figure of a man caught my eye first. Hunched against the cold with his hood pulled up, he rounded the corner and was gone before we got close enough for me to see who it was.

The former furniture store was one of the few buildings that still remained empty. Given our efforts over the past year and a half, Martha, her crew, and I had something to be proud of since empty buildings no longer outnumbered the occupied ones. We'd begun to bring the entire town back from the dead, why was I so surprised that my personal life dealt with similar themes?

"Abner Mayfield was the owner. Came from out of town, but his wife was local. I bought a nice davenport off them once. Got me almost a whole book of S&H green stamps for it, too."

Good to know, but information I hardly expected to need. Still, I let her talk. The sound of her voice had always soothed something in my soul. Made me feel safe. I hadn't realized until now how much I'd missed that feeling. Being with Drew came close, and my dad was certainly protective of me, but this was different. Her presence carried an aura of comfort and something that felt sacredly feminine. Something timeless.

"I remember Mr. Mayfield a little, I think," I said, my tone mild. "We bought a washing machine from him once."

"So many empty buildings," she gave me a glance. "It strikes a person funny to see it all so different."

We both knew her chatter was meant to distract me from the coming ordeal, so I let her speak of scandal but didn't listen too closely as she pulled into a parking space in front of Curated Collections. Too much anticipation and dread rolled through me.

"I've only just managed to patch things up with

Neena. Can you please try not to do or say anything to set her off again?"

We'd parked, so when she took a moment to level an annoyed look at me, we weren't in danger of crashing. Little by little, I'd worked at imagining her face transposed over mine, so at least I didn't feel like I was looking in a wonky mirror all the time anymore.

"I'm a delightful person, Everly. Everyone said so. Some even called me a hoot."

"You are a hoot and always have been. I didn't mean to cast aspersions on your character. Neena can be touchy, is all I meant."

"Fancy talk," she said, the lines around her mouth softening. "I'll try not to offend your little friend with my plain speaking, and you'll be there to ensure I don't."

If she'd lived, I supposed our relationship would have altered into something vastly different as I became an adult. We'd have had time to develop mutual respect as two grown women, but she hadn't lived and still saw me as the child she hadn't been around to help finish raising. I still saw her through the eyes of childhood as well, which left us in a weird place, even if spending this time with her was a gift I'd never expected and almost didn't regret.

"I didn't mean to be disrespectful." If I could have hugged her, I would have given her such a squeeze. "You know I love you."

"As I love you. You're sure you want to do this? People don't take kindly to talk of spirits and whatnot. Scares them."

I was already shaking my head. "My friends are made

33

from sterner stuff, and they've already tasted what the other side can dish out. They'll stand. You'll see."

"If you say so. Now would you rather go in and get this over with or sit out here where passers-by can see you talking to yourself all morning?"

Oh hell. I'd forgotten no one could see me, and while I contemplated her question, things got worse. "Shoot. Momma Wade just pulled into the back lot. I know you have opinions about Leandra's meddling, but you need to keep them to yourself."

"I promise to try. Best I can do."

Or, we could wait another day, but then I ran the risk of ticking off my friends for waiting too long to tell them of my current undeadedness—and yes, I was aware that wasn't a word, but some situations don't have accurate words to describe them, so I made one up.

"She's a good person and was only trying to help, which is all you were trying to do when," I waved my hand to indicate my non-corporeal body, "this happened."

"Am I the pot or the kettle?"

I couldn't hold back a smile. "Neither. You're my beloved grandmother who only wants what's best for me, just as Leandra is my second mom who wants the same thing. Be nice."

"I'm always nice."

That one earned her a cocked eyebrow. Grammie Dupree always meant well, but she didn't censor her opinions, so her definition of *nice* and mine were quite different. "Be nicer than usual."

I followed her inside and hoped for the best.

I should have known that with Leandra there, things

would go in a weird direction. Leandra is the engineer of the train to Weirdville. Probably the conductor as well. And the ticket taker.

"You're not Everly," were the first words out of her mouth when I walked in. My guts clenched. "What happened to Everly?"

Chapter 5

Jacy stood behind the counter, marking prices on a set of fine tableware while banging and thrashing sounds echoed from the small storage area behind the half of the shop where Neena sold artwork. "Don't be ridiculous, Mom. Are you feeling okay?"

"I'm fine, but that is not Everly," Leandra doubled down on her opinion. "I can't get a clear picture of who it is, but I know what I know."

"She's right," Grammie said. "I'm not Everly." If you're planning to drop a bomb on someone, it's best to do it quickly, I supposed.

Patrea stood from her examination of an antique dresser. "Very funny."

"She's not. I'm telling you," Leandra insisted. "That is not Everly."

Jacy shoved her fingers through her hair. "You two are in cahoots for some reason, but I don't have time for silly games right now."

"Be gentle with her," I ordered my grandmother. "Ask her to get Neena, so you only have to tell it once."

She shot me a look, then just yelled for Neena herself. "Okay, I guess that works, too."

"What are you yellin' at me for?" Neena came around

36

the corner wearing a scowl, her dark hair covered by a bandanna and a feather duster in her hand.

"Sorry to interrupt your cleaning, but I only plan on saying this once." Grammie glanced over at me, and I nodded for her to start, but she hesitated momentarily.

"Get on with it, then." Jacy rounded the counter to stand next to Leandra. "You're scaring me."

"Sorry, honey. That wasn't my intent."

Jacy cocked a brow at the word 'honey' but kept quiet while Grammie struggled to find a way to tell my story.

Shrugging, she finally just launched right into it. "You all know Everly was planning to see Jason Todd and to give him a chance to say goodbye to the mother he never knew."

"Why is she talking about herself in the third person?" Neena must not have heard Leandra's pronouncement.

"Pipe down, girl. I'm trying to tell you what happened."

Being shushed and called a girl didn't improve Neena's mood. I can't say I blamed her.

Looking at me, Grammie said, "Other than letting that fool of a ghost take you over, giving that poor boy some peace of mind was the right thing to do." Then she turned back to the others. "Lucy Bennett's spirit was inside Everly's body when she got ready to cross over. The meddlesome woman had no idea what she was doing with all that door nonsense. Anyway, I got there just in time to put a stop to it, but there was a scuffle."

"Scuffle?" I said. "Felt like more than that to me."

Before Jacy could ask the first of the many questions I saw in her eyes, Grammie continued, "Stupid Lucy didn't have sense enough to let go. She dragged Everly's spirit out of her body, and somehow, mine got sucked in."

"And just who might you be, then?" Neena wanted to know.

Her face a study of mixed emotions, Leandra answered for her. "Sadie Dupree? Is that you?"

"In the flesh. So to speak."

"Where's Everly?" Jacy reached forward, took Grammie's shoulders in her hands, and gave her a little shake. Something she'd never have done if it hadn't been my body she had hold of. "Is she okay?"

"I'm right here." But, of course, she couldn't hear me.

"Everly's right there." Parroting my comment, Grammie pointed at me. "And she's safe for the moment, except that she's what you'd call a disembodied spirit."

"You mean she's a ghost." Neena's face had gone pale as her eyes searched the spot where I stood.

Grammie scowled at her.

Leandra cut in, "A disembodied spirit is not the same thing as a ghost."

"Sounds like semantics to me." Patrea arched a brow, but otherwise, her face showed nothing of her thoughts. She must have been working at the flip house because she wore paint-spattered jeans and a ratty old sweatshirt.

Because she always needed something to do in a crisis, Jacy grabbed the electric kettle and went into the restroom to fill it with water for tea. "Maybe you should sit down and explain," she said when she returned.

In a rush to do just that, Leandra walked right through me. We both shivered, but they all—except for Jacy, who busied herself arranging cups and saucers on a pretty tray—trooped over to sit down on various sofas and chairs that were for sale while I hovered nearby.

"A ghost is someone who died and passed through the veil but didn't cross over into the light. A soul that got stuck in the afterlife," Grammie explained.

"Yes, we know all of that. This is not our first time." Neena waved an impatient hand.

Grammie chose a teacup from the tray when Jacy put it in front of her. "Everly went through the veil, and she's definitely in the afterlife."

Being helpful, Leandra tried to fill in the gap. "Obviously, she didn't die, which is the main requirement of being a ghost."

"See?" Jacy wrinkled up her nose. "Patrea was right. It's all semantics."

"Her body lives even while her spirit roams the earth. It's a vital difference." Leandra took a breath gearing up to launch into a detailed explanation, when Jacy cut her off.

"It doesn't matter what name you put to it. Everly's in trouble, and if there's anything I can do to help, count me in."

"Same goes," Neena put a hand on Jacy's, which was when I noticed both of them were shaking.

"Tell them I'm sorry," I said. "It seems like I'm the source of all things whackadoodle."

"I will not," Grammie ignored the questioning looks her outburst caused. "You've done nothing to be sorry about. This was my fault and none of yours."

Jacy's eyes narrowed. "Is she telling you to apologize to us? That's so Everly."

Grammie nodded while I muttered a protest.

"You tell her to cut that crap out right now. She's done nothing to be sorry about."

"I guess you just told her yourself."

I needed to talk to my friends but wasn't about to try possessing my body with my grandmother still in it. Even if I had the first clue how that worked, a list of things that could go wrong shuddered through me. You wouldn't think I could get a case of the creepies now that I had turned into the very thing that generally caused them, but you'd be wrong.

"I'm just trying to get a picture in my head." Neena gave Jacy's hand one more squeeze and let go. "Davina was in Everly's body, and when it was time for her to cross over, she planned to shut the door behind her."

"There was no door," Grammie glared at Leandra, then at me when I hissed at her. "But we can let that go for now, I suppose." She gestured for Neena to continue.

"Whatever. We'll just call it a metaphorical door if that makes you feel better. Davina was doing what she'd been asked to do when what? You stepped in and jammed your metaphorical foot in the metaphorical door?"

Grammie waggled her shoulders. "Not exactly, but close enough. I figured I'd drag meddling Lucy into the light before she had a chance to do anything stupid, but the idiot didn't have sense enough to let go when she should."

"Don't call my best friend an idiot," Leandra's tone was the firmest I'd ever heard her use.

"I call them like I see them."

"What I see," Patrea somehow channeled my earlier comment and repeated it, "is two wrongs didn't make a

40

right, and now Everly's paying for your mistake. You did this, and you need to figure out how to fix it."

Her hand going up to stop the others from piling on, Grammie said, "I'm well aware of what I need to do. She's my granddaughter. You don't think I would leave her stranded on the wrong side of the veil, do you?"

"Good. We're up to speed on the details. What's the plan?" Jacy slid forward to perch on the edge of the sofa seat and waited to hear how she could help. "How do disembodied spirits get back into their bodies? If it's happened enough times for there to be a name for it, there must be a solution."

Her phone in hand, Neena snorted, then turned the screen for everyone to see. "According to what I can find, all ghosts are disembodied spirits, so I wouldn't get too excited about the terminology."

"But all disembodied spirits are not ghosts. We've already had this conversation once, and I don't see a reason to have it again," Leandra said. "Anything on the interwebs about how to fix it?"

"Seems simple to me," Neena gave my grandmother a hard look. "You're in Everly's body. Everly needs to be in her body. Therefore, you need to get out. Problem solved."

"Been there, tried that," I said. She didn't hear me.

"If it were that simple, it would already be done." Jacy knew Grammie well enough to stand up for her. She put her hand back on Neena's. "Sadie loves Everly. She wouldn't do anything to hurt her. Not on purpose, anyway. Slinging blame might feel good, but it doesn't help the situation."

"You always were a sweet girl and a good friend to

my Everly."

I'd had a day to settle into the idea of not being in my body. Jacy and Neena hadn't had more than ten minutes. Even if this wasn't their first brush with the ghostly side of my life, it was the most disconcerting. Jacy's eyes kept darting to my grandmother's face and then away. I was sorry I'd brought more drama into hers and Neena's lives.

Leandra? For her, I was not so sorry. Half of this mess could be laid at her door for doing well-meaning but disastrous hoodoo on me in the first place. Not that she'd meant to hurt me, either, so really, there was no one to blame for my haunting issues but fate and fate didn't seem to care that my life...or death had been turned upside down.

Patrea cleared her throat loudly and pointedly until everyone turned to give her their attention.

"Assuming time is of the essence," she waited for my grandmother to nod her agreement, "We shouldn't waste it on recriminations. It doesn't matter who did what or how and when. You said you'd tried to vacate Everly's body. Tell us about that."

"I can do better than tell. I'll show you."

Grammie stood, closed her eyes, and scrunched up her face with the effort.

"Don't!" I yelled too late as her hair stood on end, and the wave of energy she generated set glassware tinkling throughout the shop. When the sofa she sat on began to vibrate, Neena jumped up and stared at the spot where she'd sat.

"She doesn't have enough energy to call the light," Leandra reached out and clapped one hand over

Grammie Dupree's wrist, then grabbed Jacy's hand with the other. "Join with me," she ordered. Her hair also lifted and blew in an invisible wind. Jacy's did the same when she rose, holding her other hand out to Neena, who reluctantly took it. With her free hand, she motioned to Patrea, who didn't hesitate to join and complete the circle.

The energy level rose to a fevered pitch. A ghostly light flickered between these women who would put everything they had into helping me. I felt a tug at my center, drawing me toward and then into the center of the circle.

My vision went hazier than before as if the veil had thickened or moved closer, but that was all. Grammie wasn't going anywhere, and neither was I. I think she realized that at about the same time I did because she wrenched her hand from Patrea's, breaking the circle. As the spectral energy dissipated, so did the static it had generated. Strands of hair that had floated up now plastered themselves to everyone's heads.

"That was…intense," Neena panted as she stated the obvious and scratched at her scalp.

"Maybe if I'd had time to anoint our third eyes with the proper oils—" Leandra began, then cut herself off when a chorus of nos hit her like a wall. Her expression went mutinous, and she waved a quelling hand. "Don't tell me you didn't feel it. We were close. A little extra oomph, and I think we'd have had it."

"You mean well, Leandra." Grammie patted her arm. "I know that, but oils wouldn't have made a difference."

"What would?" Jacy and I asked at the same time.

Taking a moment to think first, Grammie finally

answered, "If we can't bring the light into being by the force of our will, we'll probably need to be present at a passing or maybe find a ghost ready to cross over. Someone to trigger the light."

Patrea nodded. "That makes sense. You think you could piggyback off the spirit of someone who is already going through."

Grammie nodded. "Maybe. Never know until we try."

"Um," I said, wishing everyone could hear me, "that's fine and good and probably would work except for one thing. We're not ghouls. Would you want to crowd in on a family's worst moment? While they're in the process of losing a loved one? I know I don't. It's not like we have a ghost handy, and I think we can all agree that we're not willing to kill someone."

Faces that had brightened with hope fell when she relayed my comment to the others.

"She's right," Patrea thumped her fisted hand against her thigh. "On all counts."

"What about the Weeping Widow?" Leandra threw out after several theories for how to find a ghost had been shot down.

"The who?" Neena scowled.

"Ooh, that could work," Jacy rubbed at her temple as if trying to help a memory come to the surface. "She's Mooselick River's resident ghost. Everyone has heard of her, but no one I know has ever actually seen her."

Born and raised in Mooselick River, I'd heard of the Weeping Widow, of course, but thought her nothing more than a campfire story meant to raise goosebumps on kid's arms in the cool dark of a summer night.

"It's said that she hangs out by the river where she

drowned herself in despair at the loss of her husband. It's also said that if you go down to the river on a moonlit night, you can hear her crying for her lost love."

Neena shivered, and so did I. Just because I was currently a ghost myself and had dealt with more of them than I ever wanted, it didn't mean their stories didn't creep me out. Besides, going to the river in the dark in the winter sounded stupid to me.

"Or," she drew the word out long, "there's the haunted furniture store. Maybe you try the one that wouldn't require a slog through the snow during the dark of night." Patrea's dry tone made her my hero.

"The old furniture store is haunted?" Even though she couldn't see it from where she sat, Neena turned and glanced in the store's direction as she voiced my thoughts exactly. "How did we not hear about this?"

"You would if you'd tried to buy the building. I couldn't even get the local real estate agent to show it to me." Patrea's reply opened up new questions.

"When did you try to buy the furniture store, and why didn't you tell anyone?" Jacy began gathering up teacups.

"A month ago. I thought it would be a good investment." Patrea held something back, anyone who knew her well could tell, and judging by the blank stare she offered her friend, Jacy wasn't fooled.

"Okay, fine." Patrea toyed with the button on her blouse. "Nothing like ruining the surprise. You've outgrown this place." Letting go of the button, she flicked a finger toward the crowded space. "A building the size of the furniture store would give you room to expand your businesses. I figured I'd buy it, fix it up nice, and offer you a rent-to-own lease. There's plenty of storage upstairs with space enough for you each to have an office, and the showroom is at least twice as big as this."

It's a rare thing when Jacy Dean can't find something to say. Patrea's admission flummoxed her and Neena both.

"There's been so much growth in town lately, I thought I'd better snatch it up while it's still cheap because I'm predicting a jump in the local real estate market."

"Don't," Neena said. "Don't cheapen your intentions by attributing them to saving a few bucks. You tried to do something amazing for us." Her eyes brightened with unshed tears. "Even if it didn't work out, I can't tell you how much that means to me."

Patrea grinned. "Who said it didn't work out? I got the keys from the loan officer at the bank, and haunted or not, I took a look, and based on what I saw, I bought the building." She had the keys in her jacket pocket.

"That's what I call serendipity," Leandra also grinned.

"Tell her…oh, never mind." I wanted so much to hug Patrea and not one that would give her a case of the heebie-jeebies.

"This is from Everly." My grandmother must have sensed my need because she grabbed Patrea and pulled her in. "She's proud of you, and so am I. Even if I don't know you very well."

If Patrea felt a bit misty, she hid it well enough. "What do you say, everyone? Should we go take a look at the place and maybe bust a ghost?"

Jacy's face fell. "One of us will have to stay behind to

run the shop unless you want to wait until we're closed for the day."

"And wander around in a haunted furniture store after dark?" Neena shuddered. "No thanks. You go. I'll stay back."

"You both go. I'll take care of things here," Leandra offered. "Beth Ann's minding my shop."

"How's Beth working out?" Jacy's cousin had moved back to Mooselick River right after Thanksgiving when the chain she worked for decided to close several stores across the state.

"Well enough," Leandra smiled. "I'd hire her on full time if I could. She's good with customers and keeps the place tidy." Tidiness not being Leandra's strongest suit. "But I don't think she'll be able to stay in town if all she can find is part-time work."

"Send her over here, then." Neena blew a wayward curl off her forehead. "We could use some help now and again, and two part-time jobs are almost as good as one full-time one. We can work out the division of hours so it's a help to everyone."

Leandra brightened. "I'll talk to her about it, but I'm sure she'll be interested."

"Now that you've settled the fate of some poor young thing, can we get back to the business at hand?" Grammie Dupree was anxious to get me back into my body. So was I.

47

Chapter 6

With the furniture store being just down the street, we walked there in a group. Or they walked. I hovered and floated alongside them unseen while Patrea described the state of the building to her potential tenants.

Neena let out a nervous laugh as Patrea pulled out the keys. "I can't decide if I'm terrified or excited," she said.

"It's acceptable to be both," Jacy did a little hip shimmy. "I'm more excited than terrified. Just think of all that extra space filled with lovely things to sell and a proper-sized gallery with your beautiful paintings lining the walls."

"And the ghost of Abner Mayfield scaring the pants off our customers," Neena replied dryly.

"Rename the place Creepy Collections and advertise it as haunted. You'll double your business," Grammie Dupree suggested.

"Don't let Martha Tipton hear you say things like that," I said. "I had the devil's own job keeping her from trying to turn Mooselick River into Maine's answer to Salem. We don't need to raise the ghost of that idea, thank you very much."

"That's what Martha said when she tried to get us all

to jump on board with one of her weirder schemes." Unwittingly, Jacy echoed my words, making my grandmother laugh.

"What's so funny?" Patrea wanted to know.

"Just a case of great minds thinking alike. It always was hard to see where Everly began, and Jacy left off." Then she sobered. "Seems like that's the case with all of you. I'm glad to see my girl has close friends."

On that note, things could have turned maudlin, but Patrea turned the key in the lock, stepped into the abandoned store, and held the door open for the rest of us to enter. The unheated space smelled of stale air, old furniture polish, and maybe a hint of mildew. Dust swirled up from the floor in whirling clouds around their feet.

"Place needs some updating, but I can see how it could work for you." It was Patrea's turn to be nervous as she waited for her friends to comment on what was already a done deal for her. "If you don't love it, I'll find something else to do with the building."

Neena froze in fear as the air turned frigid around her. She exhaled and watched her breath transform into a thick mist. "Uh oh," she muttered just before Abner Mayfield came to the party.

Everyone except Grammie Dupree cringed when an angry voice reverberated off the walls, "What are you doing here? You think you can just come in and out of my store like you own it?"

The spirit of Abner Mayfield, an overweight man with a balding head and a thin black mustache, appeared in the mirror still attached to the far wall. He wore a white button-down shirt and suspenders attached to gray work pants. It was painfully clear this wasn't his first attempt at scaring people.

Nothing more now than a reflection of his former self, the sight of Abner was eerily disconcerting. He stared at all of us, me included, his eyes following us as we moved closer together. His mustache twitched, and his lips curled up in a sneer. Even before he spoke, his presence was strong enough to make intruders feel unwelcome.

"This is my place now, Abner. I bought the building, and I say this respectfully, but it's time for you to leave." Patrea's voice echoed through the room as she tried to be polite.

Abner stood motionless, his eyes never leaving hers, while the lights overhead flickered on in response.

"Um, guys," Patrea said just above a whisper, "the power won't be turned on until next week. This is all him."

The hum was low at first but gradually increased to a crescendo, creating an electrified atmosphere that made the hairs on Patrea's arms stand up. Dust particles glinted in the brilliant light, and tiny sparks flew about like fireflies. As Patrea repeated her ultimatum, the lights seemed to join in with an irregular beat that only added to the tension.

Ice crystals formed over years' worth of dirt and grime, making the glass sparkle darkly as moisture fogged the windows.

Abner glared at Patrea from the mirror and snarled, "What are you going to do? Make me?"

"No, I'm not here to make you do anything. I'm here to negotiate." Patrea crossed her arms and stared him down. She could feel the energy in the room shift as all eyes turned to her. "I'd rather appeal to your sense of decency and justice, but if I have to resort to stronger measures, be sure I will."

Abner laughed scornfully before he disappeared. A wisp of smoke wafted from the mirror's glass. As he left, the reflection of his spirit lingered briefly in the corner of Patrea's eye before it faded away completely.

When the others stepped up beside her for support, and Patrea did not back down, Abner reappeared on the opposite side of the showroom and set the walls to shaking while knocking sounds echoed through the empty building.

Neena screamed when Abner tapped her shoulder, but when she turned around, he was gone. Hands shaking, she pointed to an empty space on another wall where the knuckles of a hand, index finger first, pushed in from the other side. The hand formed a fist.

Neena screamed again, and so did Jacy when Abner ran his ghostly finger down the back of her neck. His touch was the cold of the freezer, the cold of the atmosphere in space, but overlaid with the sensation of spiders dancing under her clothes.

The ghost seemed to be everywhere and nowhere at once, and when he spoke again, Abner's voice was gravelly, like he'd been screaming at the top of his lungs for years and years. His laugh was deep and deeply creepy, the sound of sandpaper on glass.

"This is my place, and I will not leave. If you know what's good for you, you'll get out."

Whether they wanted to leave or not, Abner's fury shoved against the women, pushing them toward the door.

"You can push me out if you want to, but I'll be back," Patrea shouted over her shoulder. "You're nothing but a memory, and no matter what you say, this is my place now."

His creepy laugh followed the women out the door.

"That didn't go well, did it?" Grammie Dupree proved herself the queen of understatement.

Not sure what to do next, the women stood on the steps. Jacy looked around at the others and shrugged. "Maybe we should call a priest or something?"

Grammie Dupree shook her head. "I don't think that will work. His wife was a member of the church, but Abner was never religious. If he doesn't believe, using religion on him won't work." She sighed and ran a hand through her hair, considering their options.

"We could look up how to do an exorcism on our own," Neena suggested hesitantly, glancing back at the store nervously.

"No," Patrea said firmly. "I think exorcisms only work on demons, but even if they do work on ghosts, It's too dangerous to try when we have no experience."

Grammie Dupree nodded in agreement. "If we're calling in outside help, we need to find someone who knows how to handle cheesed-off spirits without putting the living in danger."

Jacy snapped her fingers as if she'd had an epiphany. "What about Everly's friend from Oakville? She's into all sorts of supernatural stuff—she might know what to do!"

"Her name is Kat," Everly said to Grammie Dupree. "She's a medium and a really nice person, but she

52

doesn't have special powers or anything. She'd just try and talk to him the same as we did. Probably with the same result. At least not without more information. Whenever I have to deal with ghosts, it helps to learn as much about their lives as I can. We need to talk to someone from Abner's family or one of his friends. Someone who knew him better than you did. Maybe we'll learn something that will help us find a way to help him move on."

Grammie relayed what I'd said.

"I think she's right. I'll ask around and shoot you a text as soon as I find anything." Jacy had more contacts in town than I did, and bonus points for not having to coach my grandmother into sounding like me.

Everyone else looked relieved. We were actually making some progress towards getting rid of Abner's spirit. After agreeing on a plan, we headed back to the shop.

"So," Patrea finally said, "What did you think of the space? Ghostly jerk notwithstanding."

Neena shivered but allowed, "From what I saw, it's a good size, plenty of light. The floors are filthy but felt solid underfoot. Lot of cosmetic work, for sure. I wish we'd had a chance to look at the mechanicals."

"It looked like I remembered," Jacy added. "They used to sell appliances in the back and bedroom furniture on the second floor."

Shrugging because she hadn't been in town long enough to visit the store while it was open, Patrea quoted as best she could remember from the paperwork. "The heating system was updated not too long before Abner closed down. That would make it about seven years ago, so still some life there. But the plumbing, such as it is, needs a fair amount of work. Electrical system is in decent shape as far as it goes, but I was thinking I'd get an electrician in to talk about a few updates. Also, there's a service elevator in the back that will need a thorough going-over before it's safe to use. I've already contacted the company, and I'm waiting on them to come out and give me a repair estimate before I start on the electrical, just in case there's something needed on that end."

Jacy looked at Neena, and an unspoken conversation passed between the two that ended with a nod from each.

"We'll take it." Neena held out a hand to Patrea to shake on the deal. "Once Abner's gone. That's a deal breaker, but we'll come to terms on the rest."

"Damned right we will," Patrea grinned. "Friday night celebration dinner at Cappy's? As soon as Everly's back in her body, of course."

"Goes without saying." Jacy's heart wouldn't let her celebrate without her friend, even if Everly could be there in spirit. A phrase that had taken on a new meaning for everyone.

Chapter 7

Back in the car, I gave my grandmother the bad news. "I'm sorry to do this, but we have someplace else to go right now." I might be dead or something, but that didn't stop my life from rolling along. "I told Martha I'd come today and help her choose what decorations to put up in the town's square during the lighting contest."

"Do we have to?" When she whined, it occurred to me that I'd not only changed physical places with my grandmother, but maybe we'd had an emotional shift as well.

"We do. Let's just say Martha has a history of going over the top, and I need to be there to rein her in." I gave her a quick description of the Valentine ice sculpture debacle.

"Okay, but when we get back, I want to watch my stories."

She couldn't handle my phone without me hovering to instruct, but she'd taken to navigating streaming television like a duck to water. When she discovered she could access every episode of her favorite soap that had aired since she'd passed, she announced she would catch up before she went back into the light or die trying. None of that sounded good to me, but what could I do?

"You realize that's...over fifteen hundred hours of television." I did the math in my head. "You'd have to watch all day every day for two months."

Apparently, she hadn't. "Fine. I'll watch one episode for each week. How long will that take?"

"Cuts it down to thirteen days."

"Are you sure?"

"No, I'm not sure. I did the math in my head, and math is not my strong suit, but it's close enough to know you won't get through them all unless you hang around longer than I'd like to stay on this side of the veil."

That got through, and she looked at me with love in her eyes and made me wish I could hug her. "I wouldn't do that to you."

"I know. I wish we had more time and things weren't how they are. Whatever else happens, I'm glad we had this time together. It's more than I ever expected."

My phone beeped a text notification and interrupted the sweet moment.

"That will be Martha. We should go. She gets testy when I'm late."

"Martha Tipton was born testy. She's a...contrary freak." She paused to get the terminology right but still butchered it.

"That's control freak, and you're not wrong on both counts, but we'll make this a fast stop, I promise. Then I think you should grab lunch at Bertino's and watch your stories until it's time to go see my folks."

"Bertino's? They're still around?" She grabbed my purse, which I now saw was stuffed with nose tissue along with my wallet and everything else I normally carried. I'd also caught her raiding the starlight mints

Drew liked to eat at Christmas. His favorites were the green ones, and so were hers. She'd dumped half the bowl into my purse on the way out of the house. Looked like I'd have to do an old lady purse purge when she was gone. Not that there was anything wrong with that. Probably break my heart, too, but if there's one thing I've learned of late, you can't stop painful situations from happening, only do your best to get through them.

"Bertie's has the best pizza in town. With the special spicy sauce, it's to die for." Probably not the best choice of words for my current situation. "And you can't go wrong with the spaghetti and meatballs plate. Or the lasagna. But first, we have to deal with Martha before another text comes in."

"Grammie's taxi service." She grinned at me as she started the car. "Where to? The town office?"

"Yeah. Well, the storage building in the back. What used to be the bus garage."

The drive was short enough that we were two minutes early, but Martha was still ahead of us. She made a point of checking her watch when we pulled up.

"There you are. I was beginning to wonder if you were coming at all. Now, I'm thinking we should go with a modern theme this year. Did you know they make glitter in a spray can? What if we did an entire forest scene in front of the gazebo with silver glitter-painted bare branches for trees, all strung up with twinkle lights."

Grammie didn't answer right away, but since that was the desired effect, Martha continued, "We have two or three of those lighted reindeer in storage. We could use those, too, and keep everything white. White lights are understated and classy. Don't you think?"

"Sounds good to me," I said.

"Are you out of your tiny mind?"

Martha's brows shot up in response to my grandmother's outburst. Mine had done the same. "Excuse me?"

"My hus...grandfather helped build a Nativity scene before he passed."

That sparked a memory. "Oh, I remember that. Or rather, I remember Dad taking me to see it when I was younger and telling me how he'd helped with the building and carving. He was so proud to have been a part of a town tradition."

"That old ramshackle of a thing?" Martha had no idea who she was talking to when she sniffed and used such a dismissive tone. "It's over here." She threaded her way between shelves and stacked bins until she stopped in front of a three-sided building made from rough lumber sitting in front of a roll-up door.

"Grammie. Don't," I warned when I saw the blush of temper creeping up her neck. Getting hot under the collar is a literal thing for redheads. She shot me a look and toned down her response. Not entirely, but it could have been worse.

"That old thing was crafted with care and built to last, but if you're going to break tradition and go with some airy-fairy twinkly forest instead? That's just...well, it's stupid."

I had never called Martha stupid to her face and had no plans ever to do so, but Grammie Dupree didn't care, and when I admonished her, she shrugged me off.

Her tone disapproving, Martha said, "Why, Everly. I

had no idea you were such a traditionalist."

"Sometimes, I am. It doesn't look like it needs that much to spruce it up. Just some cleaning and a new shingle or two on the roof. My...father can fix it, and I'm sure he'd be happy to help. Is there some reason we shouldn't go with tradition?"

"No, I suppose not, but I don't think people will be happy. We haven't used it in simply ages." Always the drama queen, Martha released a long-suffering sigh and pressed her palm to her forehead while she thought for a moment. "Not since the year Lily Evergreen tragically passed away. But if you feel that strongly about it, we can set it up this year. Pastor Paternak will be thrilled, I'm sure."

There was probably a story behind that wry comment, and I'd have put money on Pastor Paternak having something to do with the Nativity scene falling into disuse. Would Martha be that vindictive? Yes. Yes, she would.

Mollified, Grammie said, "But it might be pretty to have a few of those glittery trees and reindeer around it. Any reason we can't do both?"

Also mollified, Martha brightened. "No. I suppose not." Then, she thought a bit more and qualified, "I'll need to make a call and see if I can line up a flatbed and a winch."

"Tell her to call Bennie. I've got the number in my phone if she needs it." But Martha was a step ahead of me. According to the half of the conversation we heard, Bennie wasn't available, but someone named Scott Vestry was there and offered to drive right over with the flatbed.

"Scott's back in town?" Even the hint of gossip was enough to perk Martha right up. "Permanent or just for a visit? For how long? Well, isn't that just something? I'll look forward to seeing him. Fifteen minutes? Sure. We'll be ready."

We spent the fifteen minutes finding and liberating Mary, Joseph, the wise men, an angel, and some barnyard animals from the recesses of the storage building. Martha had a rough minute when we found the manger but no baby Jesus.

"We could use this," Grammie waved around a Cabbage Patch doll that turned up in a box of lost and found.

"Are you kidding me?" Martha lost her composure. "That's a girl doll and ugly as homemade sin. We can't use that. Have you been drinking your lunch?"

"No. But it doesn't matter. I found him." Gently, Grammie lifted the swaddled doll from the box where she'd found it. "You can calm down now."

Being told to calm down didn't mean Martha would, but before she could work up more of a head of steam, we heard a vehicle pull in to park, and a few seconds later, the knock on the door had Martha scrambling for her composure. She hurried to the window to peek out, then opened the door with a flourish. "Scott Vestry, aren't you a sight?"

Scott smiled warmly at Martha and stepped inside. I judged him to be in his mid-sixties, but even so, he was tall, broad-shouldered, and handsome in a rugged way. It looked like he could carry a bundle of wood or bale of hay pretty easily, which meant he was capable of helping us load up the manger and whatnot.

Martha made the introductions, then promptly ignored me while she got the rundown on his life since she'd seen him last.

"It's nice to meet you, Mr. Vestry." Grammie offered her hand.

"Call me Scott, please. What all's going on the truck?"

He wore faded blue jeans, work boots, and an old flannel shirt-style jacket that looked like it had seen some wear. His dark eyes twinkled as he glanced around the storage building. "Some of this stuff brings back memories." His lips curved around the stem of an unlit corncob pipe he pulled from his jacket pocket.

Vestry's manner with Martha was casual and familiar while she talked him through what she wanted. With an economy of motion, he let the winch cable out and tipped the truck bed up for easier loading. Since the three-walled stable had a set of ski-like slides and a sturdy hook already built in, it only took a few minutes to drag it up and settle it into place. During that time, I learned that the newcomer had grown up in Mooselick River but had been living in New Hampshire for the last three decades.

Martha stepped back, and I followed Grammie Dupree over to the three wise men statues to take a closer look. From their robes to their facial expressions and well-crafted staffs, I was impressed by their intricate design.

"So beautiful." She sighed and lightly touched one statue's arm before coming back to herself enough to say, "I only recently learned my grandfather made them."

Scott grinned as he admired the handiwork. "I remember your grandfather. He was a talented man. Willing to try anything once, and he didn't take any guff. Good people."

Grammie Dupree nodded in agreement and helped him pack the three figures on the truck bed with the other props for the Christmas display.

Once they'd loaded up all of the animals and carefully strapped Mary and Joseph down, Scott double-checked that everything was secure and situated properly. Satisfied, he stepped back and grinned.

"Looks like we're all set," he said, gesturing towards the truck bed and turning to Martha. "You want to ride with me?"

"Good heavens, no. I've got a dozen calls to make. Everly will go with you, and I've already sent Bess a message. Her oldest will meet you there to help unload. I can't tell you how much we appreciate your help."

"Not a problem," he said. "It's nice to see the town looking festive."

"It sure is. We've had the garlands and wreaths up on the light poles since just after Thanksgiving, so it's only the main display pieces left. Just drop it in the usual spot. You remember where that is?" When Mr. Vestry nodded, Martha continued, "We're planning to add a few glittery trees. I'll put Patricia on that right away. She's got crafty friends to help and fewer brain cells to lose from the smell of the paint."

"Did she say that out loud?" I wondered. Bess and Patty landed on Martha's naughty list almost weekly, but that was the snottiest remark I'd ever heard her make. Something else must be up, but I didn't want to delve into their friendship dynamics when I had to use a go-between. "Doesn't matter. Let it go."

Grammie was only too happy to follow that order and, instead of engaging in more discussion, watched the truck pull out with her husband's handiwork strapped to the back. Since her eyes misted up a bit, it was a good thing Martha had taken herself outside to call and issue Bess and Patty their orders.

"I wish I'd have had the chance to know Grampy. He must have been something. I mean, a woodworker who can also hypnotize people is a rare person." I wasn't trying to be facetious, but then, I wasn't trying not to be, either.

"He learned it all in the same place."

"If it makes you feel any better, Dad credits his father with teaching him a love for working with his hands, and he's carried on the woodworking side of the tradition at least. He's a good man. That's down to how you raised him."

Misting up again, she nodded and followed me out. Still on the phone, Martha waved her goodbyes, so I assumed we were done.

Chapter 8

Besides the quiet hum of the engine, fresh snow crunching under the tires was the only noise inside my car, and not loud enough to fully break the tense silence during the short drive to my parent's house. Oil and water mixed better than my mother and grandmother on their best day together. This visit would not be anyone's best day. Under all the bluster, they loved each other, but love wasn't enough to dull the sharp side of either woman's tongue.

If the thing with Abner Mayfield had gone better, I'd have already been back in my body, and my parents might never have known about my foray into the afterlife. That would have been a good thing all around, but my life rarely runs on the easy track, so why would my half-life be any different?

Avoiding my parents for a few days would have been the smarter choice, but I couldn't deprive my father and grandmother of the chance for a reunion. Whatever came, we'd handle it as a family.

"You're sure Everly wants me to go in with you? I don't want to get in the way of a family thing." Drew's hand hovered over the ignition switch while he waited for my answer.

Once more, I tried to channel my energy into becoming visible to him and failed. "He's family."

"She says you're family, and you'd better get your butt in there."

"I did not say the butt part."

She shrugged. "Close enough. Let's go in and get this over with."

I wasn't the only one feeling the nerves, and who could blame her? Joy often comes with a side of pain.

"Whatever you say," Drew reached over to offer comfort, rethought it, and pulled his hand back. The poor guy. It was just one weird thing after another since he took up with me, but my grandmother being in my body had to have pushed his boundaries close to the limit. I know it pushed mine.

When he'd have gone around to open the door for her, she didn't wait and met him at the front of the car while I followed along behind, feeling powerless. When she hesitated, Drew mounted the steps, knocked on the door, and waited while she caught up. Thankfully, my dad opened the door, his face softening as it always did when he saw me. My grandmother wasn't the only one feeling the sting of both the bitter and the sweet.

"Did we know you were coming? Or is this just a pleasant surprise?" He reached out for a hug and, having no idea what was happening, seemed hurt when my grandmother only stood there looking at him. "What? Do I have something on my face?"

"No," As if freed from something holding her in stasis, she ran into his arms and clung there for the longest time, her body shaking with pent-up emotions.

"Hey. Is everything okay?" Over her head, Dad

caught Drew's eye. Drew nodded, but his glance strayed away. Can't say I can blame him for not wanting to be the one to tell the story. "Let's get you inside, hmm? You can tell me all about it."

Since his arm stayed around her, Grammie let herself be led through the door and let Drew take her coat, but she couldn't take her eyes off her son as she struggled to find the words to explain the latest catastrophe.

"He knows about my ghosts if that helps," I said. "And he loves us. Just tell him. It will be okay." I'd never seen my grandmother at a loss for words before.

"It's better if I only have to say it once. Get Kitty, please."

"Kitty?" Dad's eyebrows shot up.

"I suppose I should have said *Mom*." Grammie picked up on the error before I could point it out.

"No need to get me. I'm right here. I didn't know you were coming, but it's a welcome—" The words died on her lips as her eyes met mine first. Mine. As in ghostly me, not grandmother me. That came next. "Sadie?"

"In the flesh."

"What are you doing here? In my daughter's body?" Mom's hands landed on her hips as she glared at my grandmother.

Mimicking my mother's stance, Grammie demanded, "How do you know I'm not Everly?"

"I can see her standing right there, can't I? What did you do to her?"

"What did I do to her?" Grammie fired up. "It's true then, is it? You are connected to the other side. That's how you know Everly is a ghost."

"Disembodied spirit," I corrected since she was the

66

one who'd used the term first. Not that she seemed to hear me.

"Maybe you should ask yourself that question. This is all your fault. All of it."

Mom's face went red. Almost purple. "Excuse me?"

"You heard me. If you hadn't played the skeptic, I wouldn't have had to step in and stop you from turning your back on your own flesh and blood."

Fury lit a fire in my mother's eyes. "Turn my back on my daughter because she could do what I can do? Is that what you think of me?"

Even hearing only half the story, my dad jumped to my mother's defense. "Of course, you wouldn't."

"Well." In the face of such logic, Grammie let her foul mood fall away. "How was I supposed to know all of that when you acted like I'd rolled in a pile of horse dung every time I brought up the subject of ghosts and psychic visions?"

"Gee," Mom can do sarcasm like a champ when she wants to. "Let's see. Maybe I acted that way to keep you from doing something foolish. Maybe to keep something from happening that ends up with my daughter as a disembodied spirit and you parading around in her skin. I guess that didn't work out very well, did it?"

"Mom, calm down." I finally found my voice, and it felt good to speak to someone besides my grandmother. "It wasn't her fault." Or not entirely. "There was a minor accident with Davina."

"Somebody," Dad said, "had better tell me what's happening here. Right now." Whenever his blood pressure spikes, my dad's hair gets, for lack of a better word, poofy. The more agitated he is, the poofier his hair gets. This was easily the worst case of the poofs I'd ever seen.

Mom didn't seem to notice he'd spoken. "Minor accident? You call this a minor accident?"

"That's enough," my father's voice thundered through the room. "Stop talking in riddles and half-sentences. I want to know what happened."

"This is awkward." Drew put himself in the middle of things. "Everybody sit down, and I'll explain." It took a minute or two to get my parents to comply, but once they had, he launched into the sordid tale of my trip to the afterlife.

"Mom?" His face a study of emotions, my father seized on the chance to speak to his beloved mother. "Is that really you?"

"Kitty," Drew said softly, "Why don't we give them a few minutes together? Everly can join us in the kitchen and fill in any gaps I've left in the story."

Reluctantly, she let him draw her out of the room while I hung back for just a moment to listen to a mother-and-son reunion that was as awkward as it was touching. I could have used one of my father's famous hugs, but since that wasn't possible, I was happy to see him giving one to his mom.

"I can't believe you didn't come to me as soon as something happened. Why am I always the last to know anything that's going on in your life?"

Poor Drew. Caught between two awkward situations, he glanced around for something to do to keep from being an unwilling spectator to family drama and noticed my mother had been cutting up root vegetables for a stew.

"I'll be over here if you need me," he said. "Not listening to half a conversation that's fully not my business." The mild attempt at humor fell flat, and being five steps away from the action didn't shield him from the dressing down my mother gave me as she came to terms with the current state of events. Eventually, a sense of calm returned, and she bent her attention to problem-solving.

"You have to tell your grandmother to cross back over. That's all there is to it. It's purely selfish of her to stay."

"Easier said than done. Don't you think we've tried that already?"

"I can't believe she'd do something so horrible, though maybe that shouldn't seem like such a stretch now that I know what else went on behind my back."

"We thought we had a solution. And maybe we still do, but things didn't quite work out how we expected." I gave her the high points of our initial experience with Abner Mayfield. "We'll have to try again whether it helps Grammie Dupree cross over or not. Patrea bought the furniture store with the intention of renting it to Jacy and Neena so they can expand, but with Abner determined to make trouble, I don't know if they'll ever feel safe enough to go forward if we can't help him move on."

"It was that bad?" Mom had been watching Drew as he finished cutting up vegetables and just went ahead and added them to the pot. When he picked up the pepper grinder and gave it a few turns, she nodded her approval and relaxed.

"Bad enough."

We'd given Drew enough details that he chimed in with a similar sentiment. Maybe because he couldn't see me, he forgot I could see him when he let his expression slip. Mom saw it, too, because she rose and put her hand on his shoulder. When he turned to her, she gathered him in and patted his back.

"It will all be okay."

He nodded but didn't speak and held on until my father and grandmother entered the kitchen.

Grammie looked like she'd been through the wringer. Her hair was mussed, and her face was blotchy from tears. I could see that Dad was also having difficulty keeping his emotions in check. It's not every day a person gets to talk to their long-dead mother.

"I was just comforting Drew. He's worried about Everly, as am I. Some of us don't seem quite so upset about the situation."

Dad's gaze traveled from his wife to his mother and back again.

"Since I'm certain I do not fall into that category, I think it might be a good idea if I showed Drew something in my workshop."

"Coward," my mother said, but with no heat. Dad's hand landed on my grandmother's shoulder as he left the room with Drew only a few steps behind. "Both of you."

They'd barely cleared the door when Mom and Grammie Dupree squared off.

"You know," Grammie said, "if you'd told me you had the gift instead of going out of your way to shield Everly from my so-called crazy notions, we wouldn't be in this pickle right now."

"Me? What about you? I watched her for signs

thinking I'd explain when and if the time came, but you didn't give me a chance." Kitty's eyes narrowed while Sadie tried her best to look innocent. "Why bother to fill her head with tales of ghosts when you'd fixed it so she wouldn't see them? What was the plan there?"

"To protect my granddaughter and prepare her for what she had inside."

"How did that work out for you? Have you ever even seen a real ghost?"

"I have now," Grammie muttered.

I didn't want to be present for this conversation, and since I also couldn't leave, I decided to end the arguing once and for all, so I channeled my mother.

Yep. I used her most chiding tones against her. I'm not proud of it. Or maybe, I am.

"Children," my voice echoed when I put some force into it. I hadn't been expecting that. "That's enough. You both made choices. Not all of those choices were good ones, and I'm the one paying the price, so quit throwing blame at each other and accept the situation for what it is, or I'll go find someone else to help me." That was an empty threat since I didn't seem to be able to travel more than a few feet from my body, but they didn't have to know that. "I'm sure Leandra would be willing to do whatever it takes."

That last bit got their attention.

"There's no need to go bothering Leandra with our personal business," Mom said.

"She already knows," Grammie informed her.

"Leandra knows? You told her before coming to me?" Uh oh. I could almost hear the whoosh as the opener broke the seal on that can of worms.

"It wasn't like that, Mom. I went to talk to Jacy and Neena, and she showed up."

"So it goes Jacy, then Neena, and then me?"

"And Patrea." I know Grammie was trying to be helpful.

"I see. Jacy," Kitty held her hand up with her palm flat, "Neena," she moved her palm lower to indicate the pecking order. "Patrea, Leandra, and anyone else who happens to show up at the opportune time, then me."

"How did I end up on the hot seat? I'm the victim here, remember? Stop trying to deflect. We've all done things we could have done differently. Can we just stop fighting and work together as a family?"

Mom rose to stir the pot. Literally, not figuratively. The pot of stew.

"For what it's worth, Kitty. I never meant to get between you and Everly. I didn't think of it that way."

Her back still turned toward the table, my mom's shoulders dropped from their hunched position. "I know you loved Everly, and you wouldn't knowingly hurt her any more than I would."

They hugged it out. The world did not end, and I realized this chance for them to work things was one more unexpected blessing from this situation. With the hatchet finally fully buried, all three of us Dupree women put our heads together to figure out a plan.

"Even if he wasn't murdered, Abner clearly has unfinished business. He's not about to tell us what that is, so we'll have to find his family and talk to them. If he has any left."

"There was a sister," Grammie remembered. "Abner had a sister who lived out on County Line Road."

"Betty?" Mom pulled the name out of her memory.

Grammie nodded. "That's the one. We'll go talk to her."

But before she finished, my mother was shaking her head. "Betty passed a few years back."

Her shoulders drooping slightly, Grammie sighed. "That's too bad. I liked Betty. Didn't she have a little girl? What was her name? Millie? Marion?" I guessed I knew where my dogged determination had come from. Grammie had at least two helpings of it.

"Mabel," my mother supplied.

"You mean Blue Moon Mabel?" I said.

Mom nodded.

"We need to talk to her, then. It's too late today. How about we meet there for breakfast in the morning," I said. "Tomorrow's your day off, isn't it? Unless you have plans."

Grammie shot my mother a look. "We can handle it if you don't have time."

"Any plans I have can be changed. My daughter's welfare comes first, as you should well know. I'll be there at seven sharp."

"Make it nine, Mom. Mabel will be too busy to chat if we're there before eight. The rush is usually over by nine."

Over Grammie muttering something about banker's hours, we agreed on the time.

Chapter 9

"Mabel's dating my boss." While she got ready, I gave Grammie the rundown on Mabel and tried to prepare her to fool a woman who knew me quite well. "She looks a bit gruff, but she's got a soft heart." I was thinking of the way she'd hired one of the most annoying women I'd ever met because Thea Lombardi had a son who needed his mother to have steady work.

As much as I found Thea annoying, she had helped us solve a recent mystery, so I'd softened toward her over the past few weeks. We'd never be as close as I was to Mabel, but it was a start.

We piled in and drove the short distance to the Blue Moon Diner. Grammie announced she could smell the food cooking before we even got out of the car.

"How's the gravy and biscuits? Real butter on the biscuits or margarine? Is it sausage gravy? Homemade or from a jar?"

"Can you think of anything besides your stomach?"

"Do you know how long it's been since I had my biscuit buttered good and proper?"

I sucked back a snort, and we left it at that as we went inside.

A few stragglers from the breakfast rush sat at the

counter and one table. Mom had, of course, arrived early and waved at us from the farthest window booth. Thea caught Grammie's eye and gave a nod. For her, that was almost an effusive welcome.

"I've already ordered for myself, but I told her to wait until you arrived before putting my order in."

"That's good," I said as I recognized one of the people sitting at the counter. "We'll be right with you. I just need to speak to that man over there," I pointed toward Scott Vestry. "It won't take more than a minute. Grammie, if you would come with me, please. I promise it'll be quick."

Mom didn't look too pleased, but she didn't argue as we crossed the diner, and Grammie tapped Scott on the shoulder. "I just wanted to thank you again for your help with the Christmas display. Let me buy your breakfast to show my gratitude."

"Not necessary, but I'll allow it. My mother didn't raise the kind of fool who says no to a pretty lady." He grinned and downed the last of his coffee while I told Thea to add his meal to my bill. "Give Martha my best the next time you see her."

"How do you know Scott Vestry?" Mom demanded when we returned to the table.

"He helped us set up the Nativity scene yesterday, so I thought I'd pick up his breakfast tab as a gesture of thanks," I explained.

"Oh," she shrugged, then dropped her voice slightly. "The people at the table just asked for their check, so they'll be clearing out soon, and everyone else has been served. The place will be empty before long." While she gave the update, Mom added a second dollop of cream to her coffee and gave it a stir. Anything else she'd have said got cut off when Thea showed up at the table with a pot of decaf.

"You want the usual?" She didn't smile but didn't give me—or rather, Grammie Dupree—her patented disapproving look, either. Major progress.

"What kind of gravy do you put on your biscuits?" Grammie wanted to know. "And is it homemade?"

"You've got your choice between sausage gravy or white. Both made fresh this morning." If Thea thought that was information I should already know, she didn't let on while she took Grammie's order and double-checked with my mom to ensure she didn't want any changes.

When Grammie dumped four sugars in her coffee, Thea cocked a brow. I took mine with two, but it was too late to do anything about it now. She glanced in the general direction of my body's belly and let a tiny smirk play across her lips. Great. There'd be speculation and rumors of my impending motherhood before the day was out, but those would take care of themselves when time proved them untrue. I'd had worse things said behind my back.

We chatted until Mabel brought the food, and Mom invited her to join us.

"I could use a minute or two off my feet," Mabel said. "Thea, get my iced coffee out of the kitchen, and plate me up a piece of graham cracker pie." When Thea began her usual spiel about calories, Mabel only pointed a finger in the server's direction, and it stopped.

Once we were settled, my grandmother broached the subject of Abner and his furniture store. "Patrea bought the building."

"Did she? I'd heard rumors someone had made an offer, but that was all." A bite of creamy filling covered with fluffy meringue and a sweet graham cracker crust went into Mabel's mouth and sparked a serious case of food envy in me. "What's she planning to do with it? Tear it down? That'd be a shame."

Mom shook her head. "No, Patrea's not the tear-it-down type. She's planning to preserve what she can and update what needs updating. She hoped to get some history on the building, and I remembered you had a family connection. Wasn't Mr. Mayfield related to you?"

"Uncle Abner was a character."

"So I'd heard," Grammie Dupree said. "I also heard the furniture store is haunted."

"Geez, Gram. Nothing like shoving the elephant right into the room."

When Mabel laughed, it seemed like she was laughing at my comment, but since she couldn't see or hear me, I realized she wasn't. "That's the story, and I'm not going to lie; it's probably true."

"Probably?" Mom spoke up.

Mabel lifted one shoulder and let it drop. "Far be it from me to discount what at least a dozen people were certain they'd seen. Toward the end, Abner was...let's just say his sidecar wasn't attached to the bike anymore."

That tracked with the aggressive style of his haunting, I supposed.

Grammie took a bite of gravy-slathered biscuit, closed her eyes for a second or two in appreciation, then probed. "Tell me more."

"I only know bits and pieces because I was just a kid when he died, and my mother had more imagination than she needed. But Maryann Payne tried to show the store to Leo once, and neither one of them would tell me what happened or step foot in the place ever again."

If we had to, I could have Grammie call Leo and ask about his experience, but I'd rather not bother my boss with anything until I had to. It would be easier to talk to Maryann since she tended to be chatty anyway.

"Dementia?" At Mabel's mystified look, Grammie clarified. "Abner, I mean."

"Oh." Mabel finished off her pie and pushed the plate away. "Maybe. I don't know if he had an official diagnosis or anything. I don't remember all that much about him except he always seemed so jolly, and he gave me a miniature dresser once. I think it was part of a display or something." Using her hands, Mabel indicated an area roughly a foot wide by a foot and a half tall. "It was about this big, and the drawers opened and everything."

"An idea why he'd haunt the furniture store?" Since Grammie Dupree had opened the door, my mother walked right through.

"I have no idea. We didn't see much of my uncle after my aunt died. In the early days, he'd bring Junior around at holidays, but my mother treated him so badly that he stopped after just a few years. If he's haunting the store, it's probably because he died there. He was closing it up when he had a massive stroke. Died right there in his office."

"What happened to the store after that?"

"Now this, I do know." Mabel's straw made hollow sucking noises when she finished off her drink. "Auntie Carolyn passed nearly twenty years before Uncle Abner, and at that time, he changed his will to leave everything to their son, but Junior died in Iraq during Desert Storm."

"A soldier?"

Mabel shook her head. "Civilian casualty. That's all I know, really. We weren't close because my mother swore Abner had something to do with Auntie Caro's death."

Now we were getting somewhere.

Mom's expression hardened. "What do you mean?"

Mabel sighed. "Auntie Caro died of a heart attack, but my mother said there had to be something more to it."

I frowned. "Why would she think that?"

"Because Auntie Caro had several miscarriages," Mabel said quietly. "One not too long before she passed. They'd been trying to have another baby for years after Junior was born, and my mother figured it was all Abner's idea to keep trying. She thought the repeated pregnancies put too much strain on Carolyn's heart."

Grammie shook her head sadly. "It sometimes happens, especially when folks are under a lot of stress."

Mabel nodded in agreement. "But at the time, my mother was convinced that Abner had done something wrong, and she never let up on him about it until the day he died."

Mom still looked skeptical. "If Carolyn died of natural causes, why did your mom suspect foul play?"

Mabel shrugged again. "I think she needed someone to blame more than anything." She paused for a moment before continuing. "But I don't think he was the one pushing for more children. Auntie Caro talked about wanting a big family all the time. It was just her and my mother growing up, and they didn't get along when they were younger. I think my aunt just wanted to make sure Junior wasn't lonely."

As an only child, I understood her thinking. If it hadn't been for Jacy and for Leandra's utter willingness to share her daughter with my family and her family with me, I might have felt the sting of being a lonesome child. Except it probably felt worse for Carolyn since she'd had a sister and still felt that way.

"Do you know anything about Abner's side of the family?"

"He didn't have anyone else that I know of. I think that's why they both wanted more children. I don't think my mother understood that about her sister. She's not very empathetic sometimes." Dark memories cast a shadow over Mabel's expression. "But people are who they are, I guess. Can I get you anything else?"

Our time with Mabel had come to an end. She had a business to run.

"I'd like a piece of that pie if you don't mind." Grammie wasn't fooling me one bit. She wanted to try Mabel's graham cracker pie to see if it rivaled hers. "To go."

Outside, the three of us sat in my car, running the engine to keep warm, and discussed what we'd learned.

"Total waste of time," Grammie decreed. "We didn't learn a single useful fact."

"Of course we did." My mother disagreed. Go figure.

"Earth to Kitty. Were you there? Abner died of natural causes, and so did his wife. We got nothing."

"We got plenty. Mabel called Abner her jolly uncle, so that's a description quite at odds with the Abner we've met. We learned that he has no other family and at least something about the disposition of the store after Abner's death."

"That's true," I chimed in before they could get a fight off the ground. "I'm not sure how any of this will help us get him to leave, but the more we know, the better, I'd think."

Grammie Dupree harrumphed but didn't get time for rebuttal because my phone chimed with the one I use for calls forwarded from my office number. When she fumbled with answering, my mother grabbed the phone from my grandmother, swiped to answer, then handed the phone back.

"Hello?" Grammie answered, and I heard the louder tones of one of my favorite tenants reporting a minor plumbing problem.

"Tell her I'll be right over, and we'll get this sorted out."

"Why can't I just tell her to jiggle the handle?"

That was a question I'd asked myself several times, but I suspected Mrs. Burns wanted the company more than she wanted me to fix the flapper on her upstairs toilet.

"Just tell her you'll be right over. It's my job to take care of the tenants, and Mrs. Burns is a really nice woman who does a lot for the community, so we'll go and jiggle the handle for her. We'll have a chat, and who knows, maybe we'll learn something that will help us with Abner."

Grammie didn't look convinced but followed my directions to the tidy little single-family home Mrs. Burns rented on Maple Street.

Chapter 10

"Her name's Cindy Burns, she works with the widowed to help them get their lives back on track, and she's nice. She's one of my favorite tenants, so you need to be on your best behavior."

"When am I not?"

Even dead, I wasn't stupid enough to answer that question.

Cindy's dog, an adorable little chihuahua mix, ran toward the door when he heard my voice. I'd forgotten to warn my grandmother, but she caught his little body in her arms when he launched at her.

"Well, hello there. Aren't you a sweetie?" Grammie let the fox-faced pup give her kisses on the cheek.

Jiggling the handle wasn't quite enough to fix the problem.

"Flapper's stuck," I said. "Tell her we'll have to lift the lid off the back of the toilet to see what's going on."

"Be careful." Cindy Burns hovered in the doorway, a comfortable woman with brown hair and kindness reflected in the blue of her eyes. "That soap dish belonged to my mother."

"No problem." Grammie Dupree snatched the end of the toilet paper and wrapped the soap dish in half the roll with an efficiency I could only admire. "That ought to do it," she handed the bundle to Cindy, then lifted the porcelain lid as I'd instructed. We leaned in at the same time, and my head intersected with hers. It wasn't a pleasant moment for either of us.

"Like I said, the flapper's stuck. But that's not all of it."

"The water's filling really slowly. Better call a plumber."

"Oh," Cindy said. "I was hoping it was something easy, like usual. Plumbers cost the earth these days."

She wasn't wrong. "There's no need for that," I said. "Tell her we can fix it."

"How are we going to fix this without a plumber?" Grammie forgot herself and spoke to me in front of Mrs. Burns.

Mrs. Burns frowned in confusion.

"Sorry," Grammie realized her mistake. "I was just talking to myself. I think I might know what's wrong." She looked at me, and I nodded.

"This isn't the first time I've fixed a slow-running toilet. There's probably dirt plugging up the inlet filter, and when that happens, the water doesn't flow with enough pressure to shut the flapper properly, so it sticks open. All you have to do is turn off the water. It's that valve." I pointed toward the shut-off that fed water to the toilet.

"All I have to do is turn this valve," she repeated after me for Cindy's benefit.

"And then you'll need to disconnect the line. There's a wrench in the toolbox." Again, she repeated what I'd said.

"Not that wrench," I warned and pointed to one with a shorter handle that would do better in the narrow space. "This one."

Fifteen minutes later, under my direction, she'd cleared sand from the wire screen, refitted the connection, and crowed with happiness when the water gushed into the tank once she turned it back on.

"Problem solved." Grammie tossed the wrench back into the toolbox with a satisfied smile.

"Thank you," Cindy said. "It's funny how some things happen so gradually you don't notice a problem until you need help fixing it."

Because my grandmother loved a good metaphor, she gave Cindy a wide smile. "You just described the human condition."

At first, Cindy seemed surprised, then she cocked her head and said, "You know, I think you're right." Reaching past my grandmother, Cindy flushed again and got out of the way. Our best bet would be for Grammie to pack up and get out of there before she slipped and said something I'd have to explain later.

Instead, she lingered once she'd followed Cindy back downstairs.

"You work with people who have lost their spouses."

Cindy nodded. "I do. Among other things."

"How would you tell someone to handle a widowed man holding on to the past so tightly he's unable to see reason?"

She meant Abner.

We stood at the foot of the stairs while Cindy framed her answer carefully.

"You can't force someone to move through the stages

of grief. Are you afraid he might harm himself?"

"Not anymore, but for the sake of those around him, he needs to move on."

"I know this isn't what you want to hear, but you need to give this man some space to follow his own journey. If you're patient, he'll tell you what he needs when it's time for him to move to the next phase. And maybe what he needs is just for someone to listen."

"I guess I can do that," Grammie hefted the toolbox and thanked Cindy for the advice before she left.

"How did you know what to do?" Grammie asked once we were settled back in the car.

"Not my first toilet screen cleaning," I told her about my work and how I'd come to get the job. "Leo's a great boss. He trusts me to run things while he enjoys his retirement, and I only feel like he's overpaying me half the time."

"Are you happy? Is this the job you want for the rest of your life?"

I hadn't given the rest of my life all that much thought, including the career portion of it. When everything fell apart, all I could do was get through from day to day, and maybe I was still in that mode. Still coasting along and trying to figure out what came next.

While I thought about the best way to frame my answer, I noticed the same hunched figure from the day we'd first met Abner. The man turned the corner onto Maple and kept going. Probably someone home for the holidays.

"Probably not," I answered the question truthfully. "But it's something to do for right now, and when it isn't, I'll find someone and train them so Leo doesn't have to worry."

Grammie nodded but didn't say anything more. When she should have turned left to go back home, she turned right and followed the main street out to the turn that would take us to the beginning of what Grammie called Memory Lane. When I was young, she'd drive me around to the places in town that meant something to her and tell me the stories of why.

"Some of these places won't look the same," I warned her.

"I should hope not."

As always, we started at the county fairgrounds that had gone unused since the change in roads took most of the traffic to Hackinaw, and the fair had also relocated there. Being winter, there wasn't much to see besides the remains of the cow barn that had been the only structure left standing until it had fallen in during the storms the year before.

"I met your grandfather right over there." She'd pulled off the road as far as the snowbanks would let her go. "He was so handsome and mysterious. I let him hypnotize me, and that's when I fell under his spell."

It had all sounded romantic when I was a child. Now, I wondered if she meant something a bit more literal.

"He didn't coerce you, did he?"

"Don't be ridiculous. Your grandfather was a fine man, and when the carnival moved on, he stayed behind to be with me."

"He started over. I know how that feels. Sort of. I guess. I mean, my story isn't the same because I came home, so it wasn't starting entirely over, but I know how it feels to change your life entirely." The rush of freedom from cutting ties, but also the fear of no longer having a full plan for the future. "It's overwhelming in all the best ways but scary, too."

"He'd have been proud of all you've accomplished."

If I'd been in my skin, I'd have blushed. "It's not so much."

"I don't know about that. You're doing good work helping Martha bring this town back from the dead. She couldn't have done it without you."

By then, we'd pulled away from the fairgrounds and moved on to the next stop on our tour of Grammie's finer moments—the house where she'd been raised.

"They've added on," I warned. "And put up new siding last fall."

"Nothing stays the same," Grammie glanced at the house as we drove past but didn't slow down until she pulled into the picnic area that also served as a school bus turn-around. Four wooden pavilions, empty and forlorn, lined the plowed drive. Grammie Dupree pointed toward the one closest to the lake's edge. "That's where he proposed," she said as if this were the first time I'd heard the story.

Grammie's face softened as she remembered her wedding proposal. "It was a beautiful night, and the stars were like diamonds in the sky. He packed a picnic meal for us. Only sandwiches and chips, but for him, that was romantic. He'd even brought a bottle of wine for me to try and a bottle of cream soda in case I didn't like it." She laughed at the memory, still slightly amused. "He knew I probably wouldn't."

"You never did, either."

While she might dump a good slug of whiskey into

her morning coffee if she hadn't slept well, and she would put away a couple of beers with a good steak dinner, I'd never known my grandmother to enjoy a glass of wine.

"He got down on one knee and pulled out this little velvet box from his pocket. I had no idea what he was doing until he opened it up and showed me the opal his mother had left him. It glimmered like fire in the moonlight, and my heart skipped a beat when he asked me to marry him."

Grammie had tears in her eyes as she smiled joyfully at the memory of that special night. "It wasn't fancy or anything like that," she said with a shrug, "but it was perfect for us. We were married two weeks later in front of our family and friends."

She glanced around at the pavilions before adding, "Half the town thought we had to get married, but your father didn't come along until I went to Harmony to get a charm from some old witch named Hagatha."

Okay, we'd been down her version of Memory Lane multiple times. This was the first time she mentioned anything about witches.

"Excuse me?"

"Oh, I know there's no such thing as real magic, but I needed to feel like I had some power over my body if that makes any sense. I've never told anyone about this except for your grandfather. My mother would have skinned me alive, then called the church elders to pray over my flayed limbs."

"I'm honored that you'd share this story with me. I didn't know you struggled with fertility." I had known she struggled with her family relationships. My great-grandparents had died within weeks of each other, not too long after I was born, and they hadn't approved of most of their daughter's life choices.

"I count myself lucky that even if he was the only one we'd have, we were blessed with your father, then with your mother, and then with you."

"You didn't think to go back for a second charm?"

Grammie's eyes widened. "Lord, no. By the time your daddy was old enough that I started thinking about another baby, that old witch would have been long dead. She looked like a wrinkled old corpse the first time I saw her. I didn't even bother going back. And besides, your daddy was all the family we needed. Such a loving boy."

Tears prickled, and that surprised me since I didn't expect to feel any sort of physical emotion in my current state.

"He's a loving man. I couldn't have asked for better, and that's a credit to you."

By then, we'd hit our fourth and final stop. The one I knew she relished the least but would not skip. The curve in the road where my grandfather had met his end on a dark and stormy night.

"I knew," she said, and I knew what she would say next because I'd heard it so many times. "I knew before the sheriff knocked on my door. I felt his light go out."

And then, she surprised me.

"He never left me. Your mother thought I was crazy because I saw him sleeping beside me in the morning, wandering around the house. We never spoke, but I saw him every day for the rest of my life, and when I crossed over into the light, he was there to hold my hand so we

90

could go together. He's the only ghost I ever saw."

And then, I surprised her.

"You took that from me. If what you're saying is true, I could have seen him, too. I could have known my grandfather. Maybe not in the way most girls do, but it would have been better than nothing, and if you hadn't done what you did, I could have helped him speak to you. We both missed out for no good reason at all."

Seeing my grandmother at a loss for words was a first. Seeing her shrink with shame was something I wished I could unsee. I also never thought I'd be upset over NOT seeing a ghost when I never wanted to see them, but there you go. Life never goes the way you expect.

"I never thought about it that way."

"Neither did I. Not until just now, anyway."

Chapter 11

Drew had already left for work when Martha Tipton called. Automatically, I reached for my phone, then wrinkled my nose when my hand went right through.

"You need to answer, Grammie. Martha won't stop calling until you do."

"I don't know how," she admitted after fumbling with the phone for a moment.

"It's easy. See there," I pointed to the flashing, green answer button. "Put your finger there, and drag it across the screen."

After two tries, she managed to connect to the call, and I got her to put it on speaker so I could hear and direct her responses.

"Everly! You have to come. It's horrible. Awful. The worst thing ever. I don't know what we'll do. Say you'll come. I need you." Martha's shrill tone made us both wince.

"What's happened?" Grammie didn't need me to prompt her to ask. Natural curiosity did the job for me.

"We've been hit. There's a thief in Mooselick River. Our little town is no longer safe. I don't know what to do."

She wasn't fooling me. For all her dithering, Martha

had the makings of an Army general and woe betide anyone who stood in her way. She knew what she should do, but it was easier on her if she got me to come and do it for her.

"Call the police," Grammie suggested in a tone dry enough to crackle.

"Ask her what was stolen first," I whispered before remembering Martha couldn't hear me because I was a ghost.

"What's missing, Martha?" Grammie asked.

"Clyde." Martha's wail had both of us leaning away from the phone for a second. "He's gone."

"Who's Clyde?" Grammie mouthed.

"I have no idea. You'd probably better ask her."

"If someone has been kidnapped, you should hang up and dial 9-1-1."

"Who said anything about a kidnapping?"

Getting to the bottom of anything to do with Martha Tipton involved a long and winding trip through the dangerous terrain of her thought processes to reach a conclusion that may or may not be important. I'd have sighed if I had breath, but this time, Grammie did it for me.

"Explain yourself, and don't take all day."

It sounded like Martha was speaking through clenched teeth, but at least she got the story out.

"Clyde is the donkey from our Nativity scene. You know, the one you helped set up for the lighting contest. It's kind of a big deal."

Grammie and I exchanged a look. A wooden donkey was missing? That was the crime of the century in Mooselick River?

"So, you're saying someone stole the Nativity scene donkey?" Grammie asked.

"Yes! He's gone, and I can't find him anywhere."

Martha sniffled, and Grammie sighed.

"Have you checked in the storage rooms?" She asked. "Maybe we accidentally left him behind." She knew better, and if it were a ploy to buy time, it would fail, but her grandmother didn't know that.

"Of course," Martha replied indignantly. "I checked everywhere!"

"And he wasn't there?" Grammie prodded her.

"No," Martha said with a heavy sigh. "He wasn't there."

Grammie looked at me for confirmation that this was indeed a crisis, and I nodded my head solemnly. Everything with Martha was a crisis.

She replied with a resigned nod, then returned to the phone and asked if anything else was missing.

"No, nothing else," Martha said. "But I have some theories."

Grammie and I exchanged a glance. Martha was famous for her theories, most of which would win a medal in a conspiracy theory contest.

"Do you want to hear them?" She asked in a hopeful tone.

Grammie hesitated before saying yes, and that's when Martha really got going with her wild ideas about what had happened to Clyde, the Nativity scene donkey. She suggested someone from Mackinaw had stolen him to put a damper on the lighting contest. Or perhaps he'd been kidnapped by a band of thieves who wanted to ransom him back to Mooselick River. Or maybe a gang tried to use him as target practice.

"We don't have gangs in Mooselick River," Grammie stated, then looked at me for confirmation. I shook my head.

"What do you call those girls who hang out on every street corner in February?"

I snorted out a laugh. "Girl Scouts? Selling cookies?"

Each theory was more outlandish than the last, but no matter how crazy they sounded, we had to admit that Martha Tipton did have a point: there was no telling what kind of madness could befall Mooselick River next.

After telling Martha we'd meet her at the town office, Grammie hung up the phone, and I could feel the tension in the air. Martha's hysterics had set her on edge, and the news of a theft in our little town was unsettling. We knew we had to act fast to keep Martha from blowing the situation even more out of proportion.

"We both know that donkey was in the stable when we finished setting up." I followed her outside and got into the car just in time for her to take off. As we drove toward the town office, we verified the Nativity set-up was, indeed, donkey-less. I kept my eyes peeled for any signs of Clyde or his abductor. Stupid, really. No one would be dumb enough to steal a wooden donkey and then wander around town with it.

We arrived at the town office not ten minutes after Martha's call. The way she carried on, you'd think we'd taken the scenic route through New Hampshire to get there.

"Where have you been?" Martha grabbed her coat and the keys to the storage unit.

"Do not answer that," I ordered my grandmother since the light in her eyes suggested she had a pithy comment she wanted to utter.

Still, I couldn't hold back a smile when she made a face at me. We followed Martha around back, waited while she unlocked the storage room, and under the dim bulbs, began searching for clues.

"See, there's nothing here." All that was left was the baby Jesus sitting on a shelf where we'd left him waiting to be added to the manger at the appropriate hour. "See, he's not here, and besides, that donkey was standing beside the manger, proud as you please, when I went home last night. But on my way in this morning, I noticed he was gone."

"And called me."

She nodded.

"Then I guess the next step is to look at the crime scene," my grandmother repeated what I said, and Martha's face fell.

"I have to stay here and mind the office."

"That's a shame." Grammie needed no prompt from me on that one, but she could have sounded a bit more like she meant it. "We...I," she corrected herself, "will look around and let you know what I find." At least the last part sounded sincere.

We drove back to the town square, squinting as the sun glared off snow and ice. Grammie hunched over and peered into the stable. Straw covering the ground obscured any footprints left behind by the donkey thief or thieves. There was no evidence to be found, and there was no sign of the donkey.

"Take a picture," I said. "So we can study it later."

"With what?" Grammie gave me a look that wasn't flattering. "You think I'm made of cameras or something?"

"They had cell phones when you died, Grammie," I chided gently, then remembered she hadn't ever owned one. "They all have cameras built in now. You can take pictures and send them to people just like those text messages we got from Jacy."

"You don't say." She pulled out the camera and flicked on the power button. "Show me how."

I explained until she understood, then stepped back to stay out of the shot.

"My brother would have had a field day with one of these," she said when I showed her how to scroll back through the images.

"Why? Did Uncle Vernon like photography?"

She offered a cheeky smile and waggled her eyebrows. "He liked dirty pictures."

"He'd have loved the Internet, then."

Tiptoeing my way out of that conversational minefield, I went back inside and took another look around. Grammie snapped off another shot, then followed me. Almost immediately, she spotted something on the ground.

"What is it?" I asked, peering over her shoulder as she knelt to take a closer look. "Don't touch it. It could be evidence."

"It's an old handkerchief." She found a stick and nudged the bit of material flat and into the light for a better inspection. "There's a monogram in the corner."

I leaned in for a closer look. LET, with the E in larger print, centered between the L and T. It certainly wasn't

Martha's monogram, so the question hung in the air: who else had been here? We searched around for any other clues but came up empty-handed.

"We should call the cops," Grammie said finally, pulling my phone from her pocket. "Maybe someone saw something last night."

I shuddered, feeling the weight of the situation settling in my stomach. Who would steal a wooden donkey from a Nativity scene and leave behind a handkerchief? It didn't make sense.

"I need you to take a picture before you move anything and get a baggie out of the car. I keep some in there for picking up Molly's poop when we're out. Should work for an evidence bag, and there are tweezers in my purse to pick up the hankie with." I waited while Grammie went and got the items I'd asked for.

"You've done this before," she said.

"Unfortunately, I have, and as much as I hate to admit it, you're right. We need to call the police. Ernie Polk's number's on my speed dial, just press and hold the number seven," I said, my voice shaking slightly. "Be prepared. I rarely ever call him to report something besides a dead body. He'll make assumptions."

Grammie nodded in agreement and managed to work the speed dial without too much trouble. I didn't even have to tell her to put it on speaker this time.

"Dupree. Who's dead this time?" Ernie didn't bother wasting time with a greeting.

"No one."

"They must be making snowmen in hell."

"You're funny," she said before I could prompt her.

"What's the problem, then?" Ernie wanted to know.

"Somebody stole Clyde."

"Clyde the donkey?"

How did everyone in town but me know the donkey had a name?

"That'd be the one. Martha noticed he was missing on her way to work and called me." Grammie repeated what I told her.

"I really don't have time for this right now. Just go into the station and tell Carole Ann you need to file an incident report. She'll get the salient details and pass them on to me."

He hung up without saying goodbye.

"Rude," Grammie looked at the phone, then put it back in her pocket. As we drove towards the police station, I couldn't shake the feeling that something bigger was going on in Mooselick River. This wasn't just about a stolen donkey—it was about something much more sinister.

But for now, we could only report the crime and hope for the best. As we walked into the station, I realized how often I'd come here in the past year and a half. Mooselick River had become a place where even the smallest crimes could have far-reaching consequences.

"When we get there, just repeat whatever I say, okay? Carole Ann Wilmette won't be joining Mensa anytime soon. And she doesn't like me much, so it's just easier if we keep the conversation to a minimum."

"Hey, Carole Ann. I need to fill out an incident report," Grammie said.

"Who'd you kill this time?" Carole Ann flipped over the printout she'd been reading as if to keep me from seeing what it said. Whatever. Who cared?

"No one's dead."

The dispatcher shot me a raised eyebrow. "Really? I guess there's a first time for everything."

"So they say." Grammie injected just the right amount of bored dismissal into her tone. Maybe we were more alike than I remembered. "The report, please."

Still staring at my body suspiciously, Carole Ann kicked against the floor to wheel her chair over to a file cabinet. Why stand up and walk when you could glide?

"Fill this out. Put it in that tray when you're done. Do you need a pen?"

Grammie shook her head, took up the sheet, and filled it out with the little information we had without much help from me.

"You got a stapler? We found some evidence."

Carole Ann didn't even bother looking up as she slapped a battered stapler on the counter, nor did she say anything when we left.

"Where to?" Grammie dropped the shifter in reverse just as Ernie's cruiser pulled into the space beside us. He nodded in our direction but didn't bother stopping to talk, which was just fine with me.

"Home, I guess. We have a couple of hours before we deal with Abner again. Or maybe we should talk to Martha and get more information about Clyde. Maybe there's something in his history that would make him worth stealing."

"You don't need to talk to Martha. I know just as much as she does about the history of that donkey."

Minus the years since her death, but I wasn't about to argue the point. "Fine," I said. "Then let's go on home."

Chapter 12

Patrea unlocked the door to the furniture store, stepped in just long enough to turn on the lights, then stood back with Jacy and Neena to let my grandmother and mother enter first. We'd already gone a few rounds trying to talk the three non-essential women into letting my family handle Abner alone.

"This is our place, and we are not giving it up to some jackass ghost with impulse issues," Jacy had said, her face set in mutinous lines. Neena and Patrea agreed, and since Patrea had the keys, that had been the end of the discussion. We would all face Abner together. I calculated our odds at somewhere around even. What could we do to him if he didn't leave? Exactly nothing, that's what. And he knew it.

True to form, he started up the second the door closed behind us. Same light show as before, lots of spooky noises and old Abner whizzing around in a ghostly frenzy. What he hadn't counted on was that we'd all seen it before and were no longer intimidated. Plus, we had Cindy's advice about just listening to him. The problematic part would be getting him to talk instead of bluster.

"Get out." His voice reverberated through the air,

shaking it with the force of his conviction.

Nobody left. Abner didn't take it well.

His eyes narrowed into thin slits as deep-seated anger flashed in them. He glided forward, his movements fluid like water, the power inside him building with each step. His footfalls echoed through the room, causing the lights to flicker and dim. A chill settled over the space that would drip cold sweat down a person's spine as his shadowy figure loomed even larger than before, threatening to engulf us. He was the embodiment of darkness and fury, with an aura that could choke out every last ray of light.

Grammie stepped forward, her face resolute. "Abner Mayfield, that is quite enough of this nonsense! This is not the kind of man you were, and you are no longer welcome here. If you don't leave peacefully, we'll have to take stronger measures."

The rest of us nodded our agreement and moved to stand behind Grammie in a show of solidarity. Taking it as a sign to double down on his efforts, Abner set the windows rattling in their frames. Dust filtered down from a new crack in the ceiling plaster.

"Cut that out." Grammie crossed her arms and narrowed her eyes. "You were supposed to cross over when you passed. I know your wife is on the other side, so why won't you go?"

Mentioning his wife seemed to bring some clarity back to his wild eyes. Abner stopped whizzing through the air and planted his feet firmly on the ground as he regarded us with a look that bordered on sad. "I can't leave. I haven't found what I lost."

"And what might that be?" Neena fisted her hands on

her hips. Her fear of Abner seemed to have diminished—possibly because she got a good look at the area where her gallery would be and, once seen, wanted the space for her own.

"Tell us what you need. We only want to help," Grammie said gently.

"There was a baseball card tacked to the wall in my office," he explained with a furrowed brow. "I was looking for it when I died." His eyes sparked again. "It's mine, and you can't have it."

Kitty stepped closer, her expression softening with understanding. "Abner, these women just want to run a successful business here, like you did. They have no interest in your personal property. No one wants to steal anything from you. Especially not something of value."

Abner shook his head, "It's not about taking my things away. That baseball card is worth nothing except for sentimental value. You see, my father left his collection to me, and when I found out what it was worth, I sold it for the down payment on this building. Then my father died, and I realized I should never have let his cards go, so I tracked down the person who had them and talked him into letting me buy this one back. He agreed because it was worthless, and I kept it pinned to the wall behind my desk to remind me of where I came from." He turned to us, desperation etched on his features, "Please help me find it so I can move on."

The tension hung thick in the air as we weighed our options. Finally, Kitty spoke up, "Okay, we'll help you look for it. But once we find it, you promise you'll move on and let us take over the property?"

"Agreed," Abner said with relief.

Patrea regarded my mother as if she'd come to the picnic without any sandwiches at all. "There's no baseball card in his office. That room is as empty as the rest of the place. If there ever was a card, it's long gone now."

"If it were, Abner would have moved on."

Her mouth snapping into a straight line, Patrea subsided and led the way upstairs to a room that was, indeed, as empty as she'd said. "Go nuts."

"Fine. I'll concede there's no baseball card in here." My mother ran a hand through her hair, mussing its perfect grooming. "We're missing something. Are you sure the building is completely empty?"

Patrea shrugged. "Unless there's a secret room somewhere the agent didn't tell me about. She gave me the keys and made me go in alone. Why didn't you try to scare me off then?" She turned to Abner.

It was his turn to shrug. "I didn't think you were serious. Big city girl like you's got no business in a backwater town like Mooselick River. Haunting's hard work. Haunting you seemed like a waste of time. Guess I was wrong."

"Looks that way," Patrea kept her tone mild, but her eyes flashed with annoyance. "You know you can't do it anymore even if we don't find that stupid card, right? I'm *not* going back to the city, I *do* own the building, and these women *will* expand their business into this space. If that's how things play out, you're welcome to stick around, but you won't interfere with them or their customers. You got it?"

Looking sheepish, Abner nodded. "I've been rattling around here alone for a long time. I'd like to move on now."

"Whose fault is that?" Grammie Dupree mumbled.

Hoping to help him do just that, we scoured the entire store, top to bottom.

"It's not here." Standing, Jacy brushed dust off the knees of her jean-clad legs. "Who did you buy the building from, Patrea? Maybe they'd know something helpful."

"Unlikely," Patrea's gaze flicked toward Abner. "There was no next of kin."

"Our son died overseas," Abner allowed a hint of sadness to cross his face.

"And Abner's wife passed just a few years after he did. Without him, she kept the store running as long as she could, then sold off the contents and closed up when the town started to die off. She moved out to Shady Acres and passed just a few months later. According to the paperwork, Mrs. Mayfield left everything to her sister. That would be Mabel's mother, Betty. But there was a small mortgage on the store, and Mabel already had her diner by then, so Betty decided to let the building go back to the bank."

"It's been up for sale—at least unofficially—for years," Jacy gave Abner a pointed look.

"Put it this way," Patrea grinned. "I let them think they'd passed off a problem property on someone who didn't know what they were getting, but I also ensured they didn't get a penny more out of me than I wanted to spend. It was a win all around and one I intend to pass on. Curated Collections will thrive here. Won't it, Abner?"

He held up a hand. "I won't get in your way, no

matter what happens to me."

"Good enough," Patrea crossed her arms and surveyed the room. "Let's think this through. Mrs. Mayfield would have been the one to pack up the office when she closed the business down. Do you remember that, Abner?"

The building wasn't heated, so it was already cold in there, but those among the living shivered as a new chill assaulted the air. "I do not," was all he'd say.

"Thanks for being no help at all." Grammie Dupree shook a finger at the ghost. "You stubborn old fart."

"Takes one to know one."

"Before this devolves into I'm rubber and you're glue, let's just think for a minute," Neena tugged her collar around her ears for extra warmth. "Abner, did you always haunt the store? I mean, since you died and all?"

"No," he admitted. "I guess I stayed with my wife at the beginning. It's hard to remember. Then I was here in my empty store and couldn't find my baseball card. I can't leave without it. It used to hang right here." Abner pointed to a pinhole in the wall.

"Do you think you could leave us alone for a minute?" Neena gave Abner her best smile. "So we can talk things through without you getting all cranky and making it colder in here?"

He didn't seem pleased, but Abner faded from view. When she was sure he was gone, Neena said, "He has to go. I'm not saying I won't want to move our shop over here if he doesn't, but he has to go. We know that card's long gone, right? I mean, it pretty much has to be."

"I'm calling Mabel," Jacy said. "She might know something." Pulling her phone from her pants pocket, she stepped out of the room for privacy, returning just a couple of minutes later. Mabel wasn't much of a talker.

"There's good news and bad news," she said.

"Always the way of it," Grammie Dupree waited to hear. "Start with the bad."

"The good news," Jacy gave Grammie a look, "is that Mabel knows where the card is. The bad news is it will take some work to get to it. The kind of work that won't make Abner happy."

"Screw him," Grammie Dupree said what we all were thinking. "He's getting our help, and he'll have to deal with whatever form that help takes. Where's the card?"

Turning, Jacy approached the wall where Abner had pointed out the pinhole. "Mabel says she and her mother helped Carolyn Mayfield clean out the store. Mabel pulled out the pin, and the card slipped from her hands. It fell between the floorboards, she said, and disappeared."

Kneeling, Patrea grabbed for Jacy's cell phone and, when it was handed over, activated the flashlight feature. "That shouldn't have happened. I don't mean Mabel dropping the card, but it shouldn't have disappeared. Not if there's a proper sub-floor underneath."

"There isn't. Not in that spot," Abner's voice made us all jump. "When this place was built, they used a series of ducted vents to heat the upstairs. Air shafts, I guess."

Excited as she always got when it came to old buildings. Patrea snapped her fingers. "I've seen that before in old houses. They put a vent in the ceiling and the floor above, then line the shaft with metal ductwork. It's a total fire hazard."

Abner nodded. "That's what the fire department told

me when they made me take them out. We added a heating system up here," he pointed toward the series of ductwork and fans overhead. "Then I removed the vents and just patched up the holes. That's one of them."

"Plunge cutter ought to do it. Good thing I have tools in my car." Neena followed Patrea out in case she needed help bringing in the tools while the rest of us waited.

"I thought we asked you to take off," Grammie said to Abner.

"Where am I supposed to go? I didn't listen the whole time."

Finally, after the liberal use of her nifty power tool and some prying, Patrea managed to make a hand-sized hole in the floorboards.

"Flashlight." She held her hand out like a doctor waiting for a scalpel. Grinning, Jacy activated the option on her phone and handed it over. "I see something." Patrea lay full out on the floor, her face pressed to the hole while she angled the phone to illuminate the cavity. She levered up a bit, then set the phone aside and reached into the hole.

"Got it." She pulled out the card and sat up.

Abner knelt, hovering his hand above the card, admiring it reverently. A satisfied grin spread across his face as he studied the crinkles along its edges and the faded colors of its print. His face lit up with the glory of that moment.

But when he tried to close his fingers over it, he realized a universal truth hidden in a cliché. You really can't take anything with you when you go. "Well, would you look at that?" He tried again and failed.

"Now what?" Grammie Dupree asked. "Here's the card that caused all kinds of trouble. You've been scaring the pants off people for years over it, and you can't even pick it up," her tone made him drop his head and look at his feet. "So what now? You want us to hang it back on the wall? Sell it to cover the repairs this place needs since you've forced it to sit empty all this time?"

"We could put it in a frame, or a plaque with your name on it and your dad's name, too." Neena offered, but Abner didn't seem interested in that option.

"Would it make you feel better if we passed this on to your next of kin?" Jacy picked up the card and held it gingerly between her finger and thumb like it had ghost cooties or something.

"Ain't got no next of kin except on my wife's side."

"There's your niece, Mabel. Over at the diner," I said, "she spoke very highly of you. Said you were always a jolly uncle to her, and she remembered you fondly."

"I guess that would be fine. Some of the other cards were worth money. This one's just worth the memories to me. Mabel won't know the value isn't what makes up the worth." Abner looked up at us, sadness in his eyes mixed with understanding. "My daddy didn't collect cards for the money," he said softly. "It was about the memory of sitting in the barn, drinking an RC Cola and eating Old King Cole potato chips while listening to the game on the transistor radio." With his face lit from the inside by good memories, I got a glimpse of the man Mabel must have known, and he was a heck of a lot nicer than he'd been when we first encountered him.

"Your father would have been proud of all your accomplishments, Abner." Count on Kitty Dupree to say the right thing. She had a knack for it. "With or without the card to anchor your memories."

"I suppose you're right," Abner admitted. "Go ahead and do whatever you want with it. Just seeing it again was enough, and now, it's time for me to move on."

"Next time, don't be such a jackass. You could have just asked for help the first time we came in, and it really wasn't necessary to scare the nice real estate lady, either."

"I suppose not, but there won't be any next time. I'm sorry for being such a nasty spook. Thanks for your help, though."

With those words, Abner slowly rose off the ground while a bright light filled the room with warmth. We all stood, transfixed, and watched as the brilliance began to draw him in. Wasn't this what we'd been waiting for?

"Grammie!" I shouted. She must have forgotten the final part of our plan because she frowned, and then her face cleared.

Abner paused one last time before disappearing forever and gave us a final nod of thanks. Grammie grabbed me and tried to follow as he crossed into eternity. I felt the pull of her intention, drawing me toward the warmth and comfort of my body while she tried hard to catch up to the vanishing light.

"It's working," she shouted as Abner's spirit released itself from its earthly bonds, and a wave of peace washed over me.

I closed my eyes and waited for whatever came next.

"No, it's not." My mom's voice rang in my ears.

My eyes popped open to see two faces turned in my direction and three still looking toward where Abner had gone into the light.

"What happened?"

Frustrated, Grammie pounded her fist against her thigh. "I got caught up in it all and forgot to grab onto him until it was too late. He got away from me. It won't happen again."

"I should hope not." I didn't have to say anything because my mother jumped right in. "It's not like we have ghosts popping out of the woodwork every which way in this town."

"There's always the Weeping Widow," Jacy reminded us.

Chapter 13

"No," I tried to keep exasperation from coloring my tone. "Click with your left finger, not your right."

"That's what I was doing." My grandmother made no such effort. "But this stupid menu keeps coming up."

I sighed. "The menu only comes up when you click the right mouse button. I need you to click the left."

This was our third time having the same conversation in a five-minute time span, and I wasn't sure I could take a fourth without being disrespectful enough to ask if she knew her left from her right.

"These newfangled computers don't make a lick of sense to me. I don't know why anyone would want to bother with all these interwhatsis when you could just go to the library." But she managed to click on the article I wanted to read.

"Oh. Would you look at that," she said. "It's just like reading the paper."

"Thus the appeal of the Internet."

The legend of the Weeping Widow, resident ghost of
Mooselick River.

For over fifty years, whispered tales of the Weeping

112

Widow have spread among the people of Mooselick River. Some think the story is little more than a tall tale to scare children, while others claim to have encountered the ghostly apparition.

The legend tells of a woman, a nameless young widow, living on the edge of town when her husband went out to hunt for dinner and never returned. Desperate with sorrow and unable to find solace in her grief, the widow took to the river's edge where she wandered, all alone, weeping bitterly and carrying a single white rose. Months passed as the widow struggled with the painful cloud that had settled over her life until one night, she simply disappeared - never to be seen alive again.

What happened to the Weeping Widow? There are several theories.

Some say her grief built over time until she could stand the pain no more, and when the next spring's thaw filled the river's banks to bursting, she leaped into them to be reunited with her one true love. Others say the young widow had pushed her husband into the river during a moment of anger, and when the guilt finally overwhelmed her, followed him to a watery grave.

Did she commit suicide? Or did someone give her a push? Most agree that the woman met her end in the dark and cold waters of Mooselick River.

Those with courage enough to brave the riverbank at night often see the ghost of the weeping widow, her white gown shimmering in the moonlight as she wails her sorrows into the wind, her desperate sobs echoing through the foggy night air.

As the years passed and the legend grew, more

and more people made pilgrimages to the river to
pay their respects to the Weeping Widow. By 1978, it
had become a tradition among newlyweds to visit the
site and offer a single rose to the river on her behalf.
Should the waters carry the rose downstream, the
marriage would thrive, but if the rose sank, the new
couple's love was doomed to end in sorrow.

I finished reading the first section of the text out loud,
then waited for my grandmother to scroll down, but she
didn't.

"What a load of utter rubbish. Who wrote this crap?"
Grammie Dupree wasn't one to mince words, but she
had me curious, so I checked the story's byline, which
she could have done herself, but I didn't point that out.

"It's an older story. Written in 1997 by someone
named Millie Nicholson. I wonder if she's related to
Carlene."

"If Carlene is the snippy little brat who used to tie a
bell to her cat's tail, then yes, Millie would be her
mother." A wry twist of her lips gave me all I needed to
know about my grandmother's opinion of Millie and of
Carlene.

"I don't know about bells and cats, but Carlene isn't a
fan of mine, and the feeling is mutual. Click the back
button, and we'll keep looking."

"What back button?" Grammie held up the mouse and
squinted at it to see if there were any labels on the
buttons." I pointed to the screen where I wanted her to
click and had her keep going.

"Stop. I think I saw something." My fingers itched to
take over for her, but I could only wait until she slowly
scrolled back. "There. Stop." The screen finally halted

on a newspaper article about the Weeping Widow dated August 2, 1963.

I read aloud:

> They found the man's body miles away from the banks of the Mooselick River, where he had gone to catch fish for supper. He'd been missing for two days when a small search party came upon his body. The man lay in a shallow ditch; his fishing pole still clutched in his hands, his hat discarded a few feet away. It appeared he had been dead for some time. He left behind a young bride, and the circumstances behind his death were never solved. Some say his ghost haunts the lonely forest, searching for his lost love.
>
> Even in late spring, Mooselick River runs dark and cold. In some spots, the water is deep and dangerous. So it was on the day the lonely bride could stand her grief no more. Her pockets packed with stones, the weeping widow walked into the river.
>
> From that day to this, it is said her ghost haunts the river while his haunts the forest, and never the two shall meet.

"Fat load of hooey." Grammie offered her opinion.

She wasn't wrong. "Both stories are lacking in basic detail, and was he hunting or was he fishing? There are contradictions. Are we sure any of this actually happened? What were their names? What year did they die? Did they have family in the area? And what part of the river is she said to haunt? We need more to go on."

"We'll keep looking. I'm beginning to get the hang of this thing." She picked up the mouse and waved it around. "What else can you look up?"

"Anything and everything," I said, not wanting to

discourage her but also not wanting to give her any more ideas. "Or just about. But like anything else, there's the bad with the good because people can post anything they want, and you're stuck trying to decide what's true and what isn't. Just like we're doing now."

Taking that information in, Grammie kept scrolling and found several more snippets on the Weeping Widow, but it was a blog post detailing a firsthand account of one man's experience with her that gave us a general location.

All that was certain, he wrote, was that the legend of the Weeping Widow was so powerful that it seemed to take a life of its own. One that still lingers in the air around Mooselick River to this day. The townsfolk eventually grew fearful of this strange apparition. Some feared that she was an omen of bad luck, while others thought she was simply lost in grief and needed help.

On a cold and windy night, my father found himself in a particular spot on the banks of Mooselick River. When a woman appeared, dressed in flowing white and appearing to need help, he approached and offered assistance. When he got close, however, the woman vanished into thin air before his very eyes. He never saw her again, but he said *to be near her was to be overwhelmed with sadness and despair*. He felt her loss in his bones and told his story to everyone he met.

Some said that anyone who caught sight of the Weeping Widow was cursed with an unending sorrow...others speculated that she was searching for something in the river but had never found it. Whatever the truth, the woman's grief touched my father in a way he passed on to me. I'll admit I found the idea of her fascinating. Could I be the one to succeed where he had failed? To offer her comfort or knowledge and help her find peace?

I had to know, so I chose a night where the moon rode high and round to light my way, and I followed the river to where it bends below an outcropping of stone.

"I know that spot," I said to Grammie Dupree. "It's not too far from where we found Delly Harper."

Engrossed, she only nodded and kept reading. So did I.

It was the sweet smell of lilacs that drew me, the faintest hint of floral perfume in the otherwise still and silent night air. Then I saw her. She was the river, the fog, and a feather on your tongue all at once, and I'm not even sure it's metaphorical to compare the sound of her weeping to a drug that slides through your veins. All I know is I wanted to give her comfort.

Creeping wisps of steam curled and spiraled above the water. The air felt thick and heavy. Black tendrils, like octopus tentacles, slithered and pulsed beneath the water. I felt the call, the pull of its dark depths offering respite from the pain.

The full moon beamed in the sky, its reflection shimmering on the river. The Weeping Widow looked up at me with tear-drenched eyes. The light of her ghostly pallor illuminated the elegant white rose clutched in her hand.

The widow's long black hair hung in dampened tendrils down her back. Her muffled sobs echoed off the granite and broke my heart. She was a sad poem locked inside a trunk under a staircase. She was the memory of a scent, that ghostly olfactory presence the trace of a fragrance can leave behind in the air. She was motes of light fading into darkness.

I begged her to stay. To talk, to heal, but she saw no reason to stay. The rose fell first. Arms spread, the widow followed, her waterlogged dress pulling her down like an anchor. The river's current swept her hair into tangles and turned her pale flesh into a beacon of white in the darkness of the water.

"Flowery talk," Grammie observed. "Ten bucks says that guy found himself a dark-haired wife."

I wouldn't take that bet, but at least now, we knew where to find the Weeping Widow.

Chapter 14

My grandmother was using my body to talk to my boyfriend about my childhood. I've had some weird experiences, but that one threatened to top them all. We'd had my parents over for dinner, so there'd been plenty of reminiscing already, and Drew wanted more.

"Everly was a beautiful baby," Grammie said, warming my heart. "With the cutest little tushie you ever did see. Fit right in the palm of your hand and jiggled when she ran."

Why did she have to go and ruin it?

And then, she made it worse.

"Reminded me of her father's when he was a baby, and they both liked to take off running as soon as you got them naked."

Gah. Thanks. I have my father's butt. Just what I needed to hear, and the way Drew's face froze, I figured he felt the same. If the man stuck around through my latest life debacle, I didn't see where I had any choice but to marry him and give him babies with cute, jiggly butts.

As if reading my mind, my grandmother poked at the loose thread.

"When are you going to marry my girl? You're a

fine-looking fellow. You and Everly would make some pretty babies."

"Let him be, Grams. You already know he's asked me."

"You'll have to get Everly to answer that question for you. I'm hoping for sooner rather than later."

"Why?" I couldn't contain the question even if he wouldn't hear it. "Why would he want to put up with all of this?" I gestured toward my astral body and then toward my currently-occupied one. "My life is madness. He should find someone who isn't always in the middle of one ghostly crisis or another. If I ever end up back in my own body, he'd be a fool to stick around."

I should have kept quiet, but I didn't expect my grandmother to repeat the statement out loud. Or for Drew to turn and speak to an area of empty space several feet from where I actually was.

Drew's eyes carried a seriousness I'd rarely seen in him before. "Maybe I don't mind being a fool," he said.

I shook my head, unable to believe what I was hearing. "But why? What could possibly make you stay with someone like me? Someone who will never have any sort of normal life?"

After Grammie Dupree repeated the questions and pointed out my general direction, Drew turned and gave me a long look meant to penetrate all the way through my soul and then smiled ever so slightly.

"Everly, I've watched you help ghosts find peace, and now, you're dealing with one taking over your body. Nothing is impossible for you. You are strong and courageous and brave beyond belief. You take on the supernatural world like no one else possibly could. How could I not want to stay by your side through it all?"

My heart swelled with emotion as he spoke, and I wasn't sure how I had been blessed enough to find such an understanding man. Sure, under everything, he wanted to protect me, but he also knew I had the strength to face whatever life threw at me. That was a type of faith I couldn't ignore.

Sighing, I muttered. "How am I supposed to hold out against the Mary Poppins of boyfriends? He's practically perfect in every way."

Grammie's smile stretched across her face, and she exclaimed, "While I'm here, I'd love a chance to help plan the wedding!"

Brows shooting up, Drew stared at her. "Do you know something I don't? Everly hasn't said yes."

"Yet." Grammie Dupree's wheels were turning. I could all but see her thoughts. "I have faith in you, young man. Ask her again when this is all done."

But Drew's head was already shaking. "Been there, done that. It's her turn now."

Such a turning of the tables would have been considered a scandal in Grammie's day, but she took the statement in stride.

"Nothing wrong with switching things up once in a while. Does she have to buy a ring? Get down on one knee? Or what is it when they have the planes fly and make words?"

"Skywriting?"

"Grammie," I burst out in surprise. "Stop!" Mortification burned a path from my head to my toes.

"What?" She turned to me. "I was just getting the lay of the land for you. You want him to say yes, don't you?

So you'd better do it right."

My forehead felt as real and solid as ever when I clapped my hand over it.

"We should plan the wedding while I'm here. I missed my chance on the first one." Whether she was talking to Drew or me wasn't clear, but her face was mine, and I know my own face well enough to know sadness when I see it. So did Drew.

"I'm sure Everly would love to hear your ideas for her wedding whenever it might take place."

"What about you? Did you have any ideas in mind?"

But Drew was already shaking his head. "I'm easy. A wedding is one day. A marriage—at least mine, anyway—is for life. So long as I end the day with Everly, I don't much care what color flowers she carries or if the tables are draped with…what's that netting stuff that looks like a ballerina's tutu?"

"Tulle." Grammie Dupree grinned.

"Sounds like hammers and pliers to me, but whatever. I'd marry her anywhere, anytime."

Grammie laughed again. "You remind me of my husband. He was an affable man most of the time, but like a kernel of popcorn, if you added heat and got him agitated, he'd pop. You never could tell which way he'd fly. Kept things interesting as I liked to stir him up from time to time. Made life more fun, if you know what I mean."

I was afraid I did and that Drew did as well. I wouldn't have been surprised to see him put his fingers in his ears to block out more information than he needed to hear. I was tempted to do the same.

Bless him, Drew changed the subject, sort of, by

asking for more stories from my childhood.

"I have a million of them." Drew's eyes lit up as Grammie Dupree launched into the description of my first steps. Hearing her tell the familiar tale—familiar to me, at any rate—I wished I could hear it in her voice rather than mine. Still, her folksy charm came through. "Ask my son to show you the video sometime."

"Sorry, Grams. No one uses VHS tapes anymore, so unless Dad converted those to digital format, I doubt Drew will get the chance."

"You can be sure I will. Everly never mentioned there were videos. I'd love to see them."

Although she spoke to Drew, my grandmother aimed her smile at me. "We had a house out on the outskirts. Off of County Line Road. You know the area?"

Drew nodded. "I spent some time camping out that way while we were all looking for Baxter Thomas."

"So you know how dark it gets in the country. You can't even see the lights of the town from there. On a moonless night, it's so dark you can't see your hand in front of your face."

Drew nodded again.

"One Friday night, Everly decided she wanted to touch a star, so she sneaked out of bed and tried to climb up onto the roof. Thankfully I heard the trellis creaking under her weight and got to her before she put herself in harm's way."

I couldn't have been more than five or six, but I remembered the incident. "Tell him the rest. Tell him what you did."

"Kitty would have my hide if she knew I got out the ladder, and we both climbed up there safely. We

123

couldn't touch a star, but I don't think I've ever seen so many at one time or felt them so close I could swear they were singing. We stayed up there half the night."

Drew chuckled at the thought of me trying to reach the stars and asked for another story.

"I've got a million of them!" replied Grammie Dupree. She went on to spin tales of how I used to chase fireflies around the yard, how Jacy and I made an igloo out of snow in the backyard, and the time I thought I should feed a family of ducks in the pond a full meal of spaghetti and meatballs.

But the story that made Drew laugh the most was when she told him about a particularly hot summer day at the lake. I'd begged my grandmother to let me swim until she couldn't take it anymore. She finally relented, but only after making me promise not to get my hair wet because she didn't feel like dealing with the tangled mess it would become.

So there I was, bobbing near the shore with my hair piled on my head, when a frog jumped off a nearby rock and landed right on top of my head. My grandmother ran down to the shoreline as fast as she could, yelling for me to get out of the water. But it was too late by then—I had already sunk below the surface.

When Grammie Dupree got to me, she discovered that not only had I gotten my hair wet, but during the struggle, I'd ended up with muck and bits of lily pad stuck in it. To make matters worse, that pesky frog was still tangled in the mass of curling red strands. When I finally emerged from the lake looking like an extra from The Little Mermaid, we learned my dad caught the whole performance with his video camera.

"I'd be willing to bet there's a VHS machine somewhere in this house," Drew grinned. "Catherine never threw anything out. If not, there's always eBay."

"What's that?" Grammie wanted to know.

"A magical place where you can buy all sorts of outdated things like VCRs and the equipment to digitize old videos." Drew's grin warned me there'd be a home movie night in our future. Well, two could play that game.

"Tell him we'll call his mother and see if there are any cute videos of Drew when he was little."

That dimmed his smile a bit, but not enough to change anything.

Chapter 15

"This is fun," Grammie shouted in Drew's ear, the wind doing its best to steal her breath and the words away. She huddled behind him on the snowmobile he'd borrowed from someone at the gym.

She wasn't wrong. Even in my current state, I'd enjoyed sitting on the hood and watching the play of the headlight on the trees we sped past. Getting to the riverbank at this time of year wasn't possible by car, and Grammie flat-out refused to strap on a set of snowshoes, so the borrowed machine had been our only option. I decided I might need to buy one for fun, though, once I was back in my flesh.

"This is the spot." Letting off the throttle, Drew coasted the sled to a stop, yanked off his helmet, and pointed toward a slash of spray paint on a nearby tree. "The river's just beyond those trees," he pointed, and then pointed again, "And that's the outcropping near Delly's old place."

"Tell him I'll be as quick as I can."

According to the plan, Drew would wait with my grandmother, but we all thought it best if I approached the widow alone. I could navigate the trek along the riverbank easier, and we also thought she might be less skittish around someone else from her side of the veil.

This would be our third attempt at making contact. The first two failed when we didn't go far enough down the trail to get to the right spot. Things look different in the winter and even more so at night. This time, Drew had done a daylight run and marked the spot so we could find it easier in the dark.

Thick snow crust made no barrier to my feet as I approached the riverbank. A chill ran through me, bringing with it a swirl of emotions—nerves and excitement mingling together. The moonlight shone down on the river like an ethereal blanket, shimmering off gentle ripples in the few areas where water flowed around and over layers of ice.

The silhouettes of the trees lining the riverbank were almost indiscernible in the darkness, but I could distinctly hear the gurgle and rush of water under the ice as it flowed downstream. The sound grew louder as I drew closer to the river's edge.

I sensed something close—something foreign yet familiar. At first, I thought it might be an odd echo, but then I heard it again—the faint whimpering of someone crying. It seemed to be coming from somewhere nearby, but my view was blocked by the shadows of night. My imagination supplied the sensation of my heart racing in my chest as I took a few tentative steps forward to investigate what lay beyond.

Focusing on the sound, I turned left and moved forward slowly until I gradually made out a woman seated by the riverside. As I got closer, the moonlight picked out the folds of her long, white gown, but with her head bowed, I couldn't see her face. Even from a distance, I could tell she was shaking with sorrow. It had to be her—the legendary ghost of the Weeping Widow. I mean, who else would be out here in their nightgown without a coat on?

Trepidation sped up the illusion of my heart beating faster in my chest. Both fear and pity for this tragic figure rose inside me to choke and cloud my resolve. The chilly night air felt odd against my skin, but I took a deep breath and stepped onto the riverbank, hoping not to startle her.

Her head snapped up, revealing alabaster skin that had clearly not seen sunlight in years. Her eyes burned into me, a force of sadness pressing on my soul. She held my gaze for an eternity before dropping her chin and turning away.

Stepping closer, my heart aching for the woman before me, I stretched my arm and tentatively touched her shoulder. It felt real—firm and solid as nothing had been done since I'd ended up on this side of the veil. When I expected icy cold from the winter chill, I found instead an inner warmth emanating from her form.

Pain and sorrow radiated off her in waves that rippled over my skin. Her distress felt like it was suffocating me, pulling me in. There were no words I could think of that would bring comfort. So, instead, I just stood there, feeling helpless and awkward with my hand on her shoulder. The longer I left it there, the harder it was to pull it back.

Without warning, she peered up at me with moist eyes, her voice soft yet sorrowful. "What do you want?" she asked. Her eyes were dark, her cheeks still rounded with youth. She couldn't have been more than sixteen. I hadn't expected her to be so young.

My throat tightened as I took a deep breath and attempted to answer. "I've come to help you find peace," I said honestly. "To offer what comfort I can and to see you safely into the light."

Her gaze lingered on mine for a moment before she spoke again. "The only way I will leave this place is by finding out what happened to my husband. He didn't come back. I waited and waited, then came here to find him, but he still didn't come. I've been waiting a very long time."

My stomach twisted into a knot as I heard the story of the weeping widow from her point of view. A sense of futility rose in me. How could I possibly help this woman after so much time had passed? But then, my conviction surged within me, gathering like a storm in my soul. I knew I had to try.

"What is your name?"

"Victoria."

"I'm Everly Dupree. It's nice to meet you. I'll do my best to give you some closure," I promised her solemnly.

She looked at me with a strange mixture of sadness and hope in her eyes, mouthing a quiet thank you before dropping her head once more. When I would have asked for more information, she simply faded away.

I swallowed hard against the lump forming in my throat—this mission would weigh on me for more reasons than one. Turning away from the riverbank, I headed back the way I had come, and that moment marked the beginning of my quest to unravel the mystery of the weeping widow.

Grammie Dupree got off the snowmobile seat when

she saw me coming. "What happened? Did you see her? Tell me everything." Her breath plumed in the frigid night air. Mine didn't.

"Let's get you back to the car where it's warmer, and I will."

The trip back felt faster than the trip out. Grammie started the car while Drew pulled the sled onto the trailer and secured it for the drive home. Once we were all nestled in the car, I recounted my conversation with Victoria and everything she had told me. Grammie Dupree listened intently, her lips pursed with determination as I spoke.

When I finished, she was silent for a moment before speaking again. "That poor woman," she murmured sadly. "We have to find out what happened to her husband. We can't let her wait any longer for closure."

I nodded in agreement, and we began discussing our next steps—where to start looking for clues and who to talk to—as we drove home under the starry night sky.

Chapter 16

To ensure I dreaded the trip to the town office even more than usual, we didn't make it out the door the next morning before Martha Tipton called. Grammie put the call on speaker so I could hear and direct her responses.

"Everly, I'm afraid we have a bigger problem than ever before," Martha said in a strained voice. "Something else has been stolen from the Nativity scene, and that's not all. What is the world coming to? I'm at my wit's end and can't think what to do."

Not knowing what to do was Martha's way of getting me involved, but we both knew she could handle anything short of an earthquake on her own.

"Can you come? I need your help."

But the queen of drama wouldn't be happy unless she had someone to share the chaos with. Since I'd moved back to town, that someone had become me.

I sighed and rubbed my temples. This was the second time something had gone missing from the display, and I was beginning to think it wasn't kids playing a prank.

"Ask her what's missing," I said, but when Grammie opened her mouth to do so, I held up a hand to stop her. "Never mind. It doesn't matter. Just tell her I'm on my way.

"Sure, Martha," Grammie said reluctantly. "I'll be there as soon as I can."

"Don't take too long. We need all the help we can get if we're going to catch whoever's behind this." The call went dead as Martha hung up without saying goodbye. Grammie scowled at the phone.

"She always did think she was in charge of every little thing."

"Anything that gets done in town, you can pretty much be sure she's the person behind it. I've been helping her for over a year and haven't spoken ten words to any of the Selectmen...or women...not that the terminology matters. Martha runs that office like a general directs troops."

Grammie chuckled at my comment, but my mind was still on the missing display items. It wasn't the first time something had been stolen already this year, but Martha seemed more upset than before. I wondered if the thief had gotten bolder or if Martha was just feeling particularly overwhelmed.

As we made our way to the town office, I couldn't help but wonder if the thefts were related to using some of the older decorations. If so, this was all my fault. Or Grammie Dupree's, if you wanted to get technical. But that didn't really make sense. Then again, stealing things that belonged to others didn't make sense to me at all, so it was probably a mindset thing.

When we arrived at the office, Martha was waiting for us outside. She looked even more frazzled than usual and had bags under her eyes. She must have been losing sleep over the thefts.

"Thank goodness you're here," she said, climbing into

the backseat. Apparently, we were driving over to look at the display. "Someone took the Bessie."

Grammie frowned. "The cow? That's terrible."

Martha nodded, her eyes wide. "I know. And it's not just Bessie, either. Someone also stole a garland," We'd pulled into the town's square by then. It wasn't more than a two-minute drive. Martha bounced in her seat, pointing to the space between two light poles where the garland should have been hanging. "It was there last night, but it's gone now. It's like they're targeting the most important symbols of the season."

Grammie Dupree made a tutting noise. "This is why we can't have nice things."

I couldn't help but roll my eyes. "It's just a garland. It's not like someone stole the Star of Bethlehem. Maybe it blew away."

I didn't mean for the comment to be repeated. Mainly because Martha hearing it resulted in exactly what I'd been trying to avoid. She got huffy.

"It's the principle of the thing!" Martha snarled. "And it's not just the garland. Someone tried to break into the storage room the other day."

I raised an eyebrow. "Ask her if it could be kids playing pranks."

"No!" Martha insisted. "These thefts are a deliberate ploy to undermine me. Someone is trying to ruin Christmas for the whole town."

I sighed, hoping Martha was wrong and this was only a prank. What we ddn't need was someone deliberately and maliciously trying to steal Christmas.

"Tell her we'll figure this out," I said, trying to sound reassuring. "But we need to start looking for clues."

Martha nodded, her expression still tense. "I've already called the police, but I don't think Ernie is taking this seriously. He thinks it's just kids, too. And that idiot dispatcher of his suggested it might be the Grinch."

"Well, we'll show them that it's not," Grammie said, patting Martha's hand. "We'll find the thief and ensure they're brought to justice."

I couldn't help but smile at Grammie's determination. For a woman in her seventies, she was still as feisty as ever. Then again, she was in my body, so it was a case of the spirit being willing while the flesh wasn't weak. Bonus for her, not so great for me.

"Let's start by looking for footprints or any other evidence around the display," I suggested, hoping to steer the conversation away from Martha's frustration with Ernie Polk before she got annoyed enough to call him or something. Dealing with him and Martha at the same time wasn't on my list of fun things to do.

Grammie nodded, and we all began to search the area for any signs of the thief. As we looked, I couldn't think of a single reason why anyone would want some manky old wooden animals badly enough to steal them, and what did the missing garland have to do with anything?

"Tell her we should think about putting a webcam up somewhere. A twenty-four-hour live feed would be a good thing to have on the town website, especially when there's an event going on. Plus, if people knew they might be caught on camera, they'd be less likely to steal random farm animals from the Nativity display."

"What's a webcam with a twenty-four-hour live feed?" Forgetting it wasn't just the two of us, Grammie asked a question Martha assumed was meant for her.

"It's a fantastic idea, is what it is. I can't believe I didn't think of it myself." Forgetting about evidence, of which there was none to be found anyway, Martha circled in place, looking for possible camera locations. "There's extra cash in the discretionary funds thanks to our mysterious benefactor. I'll talk to your father about it. Seems like a good project for one of his classes."

"My father?" Grammie realized her mistake fairly quickly this time. "Right. Of course, with his kids and all. Sure, that works. I'll make the call and get him on board."

Martha looked at her more closely than I'd have liked, but since my grandmother hadn't said anything too out there, we shrugged and bundled into the car to head back to the town office. Inspecting the scene of the thefts hadn't been the only thing on our to-do list for the day. But when we tried to search through death records for the mysterious Victoria, we struck out in a major way.

"Towns haven't kept death records since the state office opened in 1892, so if you're looking for someone who died after that, you'll need to go to Augusta. Give them the full name and date of birth or death, pay the fee, and you can have a copy of the records. Then again, if you know the death date, you might find something in the town reports. We always put a memorial in the back."

"Would that tell cause of death?"

"It might. They treated the town report more like a newspaper edition until the early 1950s, with little articles of interest and such. Why the sudden interest in distant deaths? Are you rethinking my idea about playing up Mooselick River's haunted past?"

"What a damn fool idea." You gotta love it when the person inhabiting your body has no filter between their brain and mouth. Or maybe you don't. I certainly didn't.

"Grammie. Be nice." I got her to hush up, but Martha's warmth had flown, and the look in her eyes when she showed us the collection of town reports wasn't very friendly. The sooner I got my body back, the better, but I'd begun running a mental list of people with ruffled feathers I'd have to smooth over.

Scanning through twenty years' worth of town reports didn't make a dent in the task and didn't add anything to our store of knowledge. We didn't find Victoria's last name, her husband's first name, or where his body had been found. Or where he'd died if those two places weren't the same. It was just more variations on the tragic theme of a widow who pined for her lost love and then took her own life. Poor William got the short end of the reporting stick.

Martha accepted our thanks with a certain coldness that said I'd not been forgiven, and we headed back out to the car.

"Well, that was a dead end."

Grammie thought I was making a pun and found it amusing.

"Speaking of the dead," she said as if we hadn't been talking about that very thing for literally days. "I think we should visit the cemetery."

"Why? It's off-season. Closed."

She shrugged. "I want to visit your grandfather, and while we're there, we might find out something about the widow."

Who was I to argue with that logic? Besides, she had control of the body. I couldn't stop her if I wanted to, so we went.

Chapter 17

"Do we really have to do this now? We could drive to Augusta and pay to scan through the death records. We'd be more likely to find useful information there than wandering through a cemetery in the snow."

"Didn't you listen to what Martha said? You need the full name and date of death to get access. We don't have those yet." Grammie pulled on a pair of warm gloves, dragged a hat over wayward curls, got out of the car, and tested her weight on the packed snow. The crust gave under her feet, but not enough to hamper movement, so she climbed the fence and headed for the first gravestone.

"Do you see that," she pointed to the text carved into granite and read the inscription out loud. "Beloved Son. What does that tell you?"

"That someone died too young. I don't see the point."

There's nothing like getting an eye-roll from your grandmother.

"Beloved son. That tells me this boy was buried by at least one of his parents."

"Okay. I don't see how that helps us."

I got the eye roll a second time.

"It doesn't, but if we find Victoria's grave, and if

there's an inscription, and if her husband is buried nearby, we might learn something about their family life. You get it now? What if her husband didn't die? What if he bumped her off and then went on his merry way?"

"That doesn't make sense, but I see what you're getting at. Let's get this over with." I would have followed her into hell anyway, and the cold didn't bother me, so I guessed it was time to shut up and do as I was told.

We trudged through the snow, a crisp white blanket that glittered in the sun. Every marker we passed felt like a story of love, courage, and devotion. Some were remembered with wreaths or plastic flowers, while other graves lay bare as if forgotten in time, but all of them contained tales of life and death intertwined together in a circle that could never be broken.

My grandmother was one who believed in omens and symbols. She paused for reflection at every grave we encountered, her weathered fingers tracing carvings with reverence. When she came to my grandfather's, one with a dove, a symbol of peace, hope, and redemption even after death, she said softly, "He would have been proud of you."

The calmness of that cemetery was overwhelming; it brought home the fragility of life and mortality. Even in tragedy, there can be beauty and respect when honoring our loved ones, and no matter what, we must keep living our lives with courage and strength. Searching for Victoria's grave was a reminder of this lesson. I guessed I was glad we'd come.

I still didn't think the trip would be useful, but there

were worse things to do with an hour.

While Grammie continued to chat with her husband's grave, I wandered as if drawn to the older sections where decades had passed since anyone had left flowers. Maybe it was the sense of peace, or perhaps it was the fact that I'd felt such a kinship with the widow, but I knew I had the right one when I saw the name Victoria etched in old granite.

"I found her," I yelled, and while I waited for my grandmother to join me, I began to feel as if someone's eyes were on my back. Not possible, I thought, unless it's another ghost. When something dark fluttered in my peripheral vision, I turned but saw nothing except for my approaching grandmother.

That she held back a smirk was something I could ignore. A blanket of pure white snow covered Victoria's grave and her husband's as well. I could sense a solemn power in the air and whispered, "It feels like we're standing in a sacred space. We should be quiet."

Grammie nodded and stepped closer to read the epitaph on their tombstone - Victoria Eastman; beloved wife of William Eastman; together in life, and now together in death.

"She died three months after him," I heard Grammie murmur under her breath, the tears streaming down her face sparkling in the pale winter sun. The level of her emotions took me a little by surprise. Maybe she wasn't any happier being in my body than I was out of it.

"But they aren't together yet, are they?" I asked, my voice shaking with emotion.

Grammie lifted her chin and looked me straight in the eye. "Not yet," she answered with conviction.

"But...we'll make sure that changes, won't we?"

"We will," I agreed. "Now, take a picture of the gravestone so we have it for our records."

So what if I broke the mood? The cold northern breeze caressed us as we silently said our goodbyes to Victoria before walking back to the car. Despite the sorrowful circumstances that brought us there, peace glimmered within us like stars on a winter night.

"Death is part of life," Grammie said quietly as a snowflake settled on her shoulder. "It's something that can't be avoided or denied." She paused to look up at the clouds above before pulling away from the cemetery with a heavy heart. "It's hard to understand how two lives could be cut so tragically short."

I nodded my agreement.

"What next?"

"Research," I answered. "Mom's at the library. Might as well stop in there as go home."

When we passed the Nativity scene, we both glanced over to see if anything else had gone missing. She waved at Scott Vestry, who had, it seemed, had the same idea, then swerved to the wrong side of the road, put down her window, and called to him.

"Everything okay?"

"Looks to be. I was just passing by and thought I'd check." He tipped us a two-fingered wave, and she pulled back onto the road.

Chapter 18

"Left click, Sadie. Not right." My mother stood on Grammie Dupree's left while I looked over her shoulder from the right. "That's your index finger."

"You mean this one?" Turning, Sadie held up a finger that was not her index and earned one of Kitty's bland stares. Deeming it wise, I kept my mouth firmly shut. Let them fight it out, and I'd happily stay off both of their lists. Win for me.

"I could do it faster," Mom offered, earning herself a thousand-yard stare. Yeah, these two were oil and water. Or maybe oil and vinegar. If you shook them up enough and added some seasoning, they made a great team. I could have gone for a good salad right about then and almost felt my stomach rumble.

"Sooo. I told you I could do it," Grammie turned to me, beaming with pride. "I found William Eastman."

"Looks like his death is a bit of a mystery." Mom bent down to read out loud:

A shocking discovery was made in the forest near the small town of Mooselick River on Tuesday when a small group of loggers discovered the body of a man slumped against a maple tree, his limbs still in the awkward postures of death. The deceased was identified as William Eastman, a local man who left his home earlier that day.

Sheriff Duncan and his deputies have yet to determine the man's cause of death and have not ruled out foul play. Eastman left behind his grieving bride of seven months, who is not considered a suspect. No clues have been discovered, but the police are seeking further information regarding the circumstances of Eastman's death.

"I have questions," Grammie said. "What's the "awkward postures of death" supposed to mean?"

"I know, right?" I said. "That's a weird turn of phrase when the rest seems fairly normal."

My mom, no longer content to sit through another hunt and peck typing session, keyed William Eastman's name into her phone's search bar.

"There are a few instances of that article on the web, but nothing else so far as I can see."

"Search for something like ghost man haunts forest or woods in Mooselick River."

She did and found a few more results than before.

"Looks like the Weeping Widow had more coverage, but then, you have to figure that being on the river walk trail, she's easier to run across than he is. I'm surprised more people haven't reported sightings of Victoria or William since Shady Acres opened."

"She doesn't show herself to everyone and only walks at night," Grammie said. "And there are none so blind as those who will not see the spirits surrounding them."

"I think that's a perversion of the phrase, but I won't disagree with the sentiment." Mom turned her phone so I could see the screen. "Only one result looks like a first-hand story of an encounter with William's ghost."

One was better than none, and to get Victoria to move on, we had to find out what happened to William.

"Read it to me."

"Better yet," Mom gently nudged Grammie Dupree over to the left and slid the keyboard and mouse a bit to the right so she could type in the website address.

"Hey, that's the same blog post we saw before. How did we miss a blog post about the husband?"

"We didn't." Now that the site was up, Grammie returned to her former spot and grabbed for the mouse. She hit the scroll wheel to navigate to the bottom of the page. "We never read the comments, and it's buried in there." One click and the comment filled the screen.

"Okay! This is more like it."

I read the comment aloud, my voice quivering with excitement.

"My name is John, and I had the most peculiar experience several years ago. I was walking in the woods near the town of Mooselick River when I felt a chill breeze and heard a voice call out to me. The man said his name was William Eastman and asked for help finding his way back home to his wife. He seemed confused as if he didn't know how he got there or what had happened to him. I tried to get him to follow me back to the road, but he just kept saying he had to get home. I reached out to grab his arm because he didn't look steady on his feet, and my hand went right through. When I realized he was a ghost, I didn't see how to help him, so I left him in peace and went on my way. It was like his death was a mystery, even to him."

Grammie Dupree made the sign of the cross as she spoke. "Those poor kids. All they wanted to do was spend a lifetime together, and they're stuck with an eternity apart. We need to discover what became of William Eastman so we can give them both the end they deserve."

I nodded my head, feeling a surge of responsibility course through me. There was more to this than getting me back in my body. We couldn't simply abandon the Weeping Widow's husband to more time spent lost and disoriented. We had to find out what happened to him and grant him peace.

"I'm all for that," Mom spoke up. "but *the woods near the town of Mooselick River* doesn't give us nearly a good enough description of where to find William Eastman. We need more information about both of them, I think."

But something had been niggling at me since we'd found the headstone.

"The name Eastman. It's been bugging me since we left the cemetery, but now I realize why. I know someone else with that last name. I wonder if he's a relative."

Even from the wrong side of the veil, I felt the perking up of both their moods. "Really? Who?"

"His name's Adam. He works in the kitchen of Cappy's Tavern. He's a nice guy. Might be worth going in for lunch."

"Do they still make the best beer-battered haddock in the county?"

"Yes, Ma'am, they do. I go there most Friday nights with my friends."

"I do feel peckish," Grammie said. "Maybe we'll stop in for a bite on our way home."

Not a bad idea. I missed food, though, so watching her eat my favorite meal wouldn't be much fun.

"I'll confess to feeling envious since it's been a while since I ate at Cappy's, and I hate to miss out on the fun." It was a rare thing to see my mother pout, but she had to stay at the library until the end of her shift.

"Next time." Grammie didn't seem to notice or care if her daughter-in-law felt left out.

"You'll have to be on your best behavior," I warned as we headed to the car. Adam's not a close enough friend to know about my ghostly adventures, so we'll have to be careful how we approach the subject."

She nodded, but I worried her careful and mine were not the same. What could I do in any case? She had control of my body. The rest of me was just along for the ride.

When we arrived, Grammie Dupree peered around the tavern, a space crowded with tables but very few people on a Wednesday just before noon.

"It looks just how I remember it," she said.

"Some things never change. Sit at the bar," I said when she headed toward one of the tables. "There's a window near the one end that overlooks the kitchen, and Adam will bring your food out if you do, but if you take a table, it will be Miranda or whoever else is serving today."

When Grammie gave me a look, I shrugged. "Not my first time having lunch here." I usually went to the Blue Moon Diner, but I intended to steer clear of that place while I wasn't in charge of my body. After the first visit, I realized there were too many people and chances she'd let something slip that I'd have to explain later. If there *was* a later.

I had to shut down that type of negative thinking. We'd find a way for her to move on, and I would get my body back. I had to believe that.

"That's Adam there. Looks like he's flying solo today."

"Hey, Everly. How's it going?" Adam said when my grandmother slid onto one of the barstools. "Miranda's on break, and Milo had his final checkup today. He's expecting to get a clean bill of health so his wife will let him go back to full-time hours."

"Ask him how Milo's feeling. He got bashed on the head a few weeks ago."

"I know," Grammie said to me, then realized she'd made a mistake when Adam gave her a look. "Sorry, I just meant I'd heard he was feeling better."

Nice save.

"He was lucky. Anyway, what can I get you?"

She ordered the haddock lunch plate, and while he returned to the kitchen, she muttered to me, "I told you I've been keeping an eye on you from the other side."

"Seems like you'd know how to use a cell phone, then," I gave her back the same snippy attitude she'd used with me. Not a tone I'd have ever used with her when she'd been alive. "Sorry. All of this stresses me out."

"Understandable." She forgave easily, at least, and kept up a bit of small talk with Adam while he cooked her fish. When he returned to plop the plate in front of her, she all but hummed with anticipation.

"Looks good. Got any vinegar to go with those fries?"

Adam's forehead wrinkled. "I thought you were a

ketchup girl." But he grabbed a bottle of malt vinegar for her and pulled out a couple of lemons while she liberally doused her fries.

He was right, though I generally went for the onion rings in any case.

"Er," she said. "I thought I'd try something different today. This is how my grandmother likes her fries, and I've been thinking about her a lot lately."

"Good segue," I said.

She gave me a brief nod to acknowledge the compliment. "In fact, I was just at the cemetery. I like to visit her grave sometimes, and I noticed Eastmans buried nearby. Any relation of yours? I believe the names were Victoria and William."

In the middle of slicing his knife through a lemon for garnish, Adam paused, his face turning slightly red. "Oh. You mean great-aunt Victoria?"

Grammie nodded, her mouth too full of haddock to speak.

"You know the story about her, I assume, or else you wouldn't ask."

She swallowed hastily. "Just curious. I'd forgotten all about her until I noticed that headstone and it sparked a memory. They used to tell campfire stories about her when I was in Girl Scouts."

"Probably still do." Adam went back to his chopping and slicing. "Her story was tragic, but what's funny is everyone tells how someone else saw her. Not a single person in our family ever had a first-hand encounter with her. It's all hearsay."

Half the food on her plate gone, Grammie Dupree shifted her attention from food to give it fully to him.

"The best ghost stories always are."

"I suppose so. I've fished that area of the river a few times, and while I've never had what you'd call an encounter, I've felt like she might be watching me a time or two. Like a tickle on the back of your neck, you know?"

"I do," I said before she did. "I know exactly how that feels. It's creepy."

"What about William? There have been sightings of him, too, but no one seems to know where his ghost hangs out. Would you or anyone in your family know where his body was found?"

"Sure do." Adam slid the lemon slices into a glass bowl with a plastic lid, which he stashed in the refrigerator below the bar top. "When did you turn into one of those ghost hunter types?"

"Tell him the story came up while we were getting things ready for the lighting contest, and you found it interesting."

She did, and I think he believed her.

"Doesn't matter anyway. You know that assisted living facility, Shady something?"

Unfortunately, I did. Shady Acres.

"They dug their duck pond on the spot where William Eastman died."

In my head, I calculated the distance between the river and the duck pond. "What was he doing way out there if he'd gone fishing?"

Adam shrugged. "That's part of the mystery. No one knows what happened to him that night. Only that he'd been missing for a couple of days when some loggers found his body in an area where they'd been cutting

149

wood."

"Cause of death?" Grammie grabbed the vinegar bottle again and doused the next layer of fries. I caught a whiff of the sharp tang and realized I could smell things. A little, at least. Was this helpful information? I had no idea. For all I knew, all ghosts could smell stuff. I'd have to ask the next one I ran into, I supposed. Add that to my mental checklist. Right after I get back in my body and never let anyone touch my third eye again.

"Someone bashed him on the back of the head with a rock."

"Murder?" Grammie Dupree perked up. "Why are we just hearing about this now?"

"Because the official cause was listed as *death by misadventure.* Whatever that means."

Having done some research in this line of things, I said, "It means the killer made it look like an accident or that there wasn't enough evidence to tie the death to a local suspect, and whoever was in charge didn't have the means, interest, or ability to pursue the case."

Grammie repeated what I'd said, and Adam nodded. "Sounds about right. I only know what came down through family stories, but he'd suffered multiple blows to the head, so it can't have been an accident."

Since there didn't seem to be anything else he could add to the conversation, Adam boxed up the rest of Grammie's lunch while she fumbled through my purse for money.

Outside in the car, she started the engine, then turned to me. "Thoughts?"

"I have a few. You're not dressed for a hike, so you can sit in the car while I see if I can scare up old William

150

and get him to follow me back to the river."

"You really think I'll sit in the car while you have all the fun?"

"What I think is that you love me too much to risk losing one of my toes to frostbite."

"Fine." She turned toward home. "We'll compromise. I'll go home and change into warmer clothes, and then, we'll see about this duck pond ghost."

I wouldn't be able to stop her, so I didn't bother to try. "I thought compromise meant both people get something out of a deal. This seems more like you getting your way."

"If you're looking for an apology, it's not coming."

When we got home, she stashed the leftovers and let the dog out to pee before heading to the bedroom for warmer things to wear.

"Let's take Molly. She could do with a run, and she loves to ride in the car." And she could go for help if Grammie took a fall.

Grammie's stocking-covered feet made almost no sound as she walked to my closet, rummaging through my clothes. Her fingers settled on a chunky knit sweater and pants with a flannel lining for extra warmth. She laced a pair of winter boots against the cold, snuggled a down parka over it all, and grabbed Molly's leash from the hook by the door. "Let's do this."

The poor pup hadn't fully adjusted to our weird situation, but today was different; Molly wagged her tail vigorously as soon as Grammie touched the leash.

The woman had more energy than I ever did, and it made me smile.

Chapter 19

With Grammie driving, we pulled into the facility where I'd once solved a missing persons case and broken up a drug ring. For days, I had volunteered here and hadn't felt so much as a tiny tingle from William. Why did I think now would be different? Who knew? But if I wanted to learn more about the old ghost, this was the place to be.

When she would have pulled into one of the visitor spaces, I directed Grammie toward the employee lot behind the main building. A brisk winter wind blew through my grandmother's hair as we walked. The sun played peek-a-boo behind the clouds, alternately sparking glares of light off the frozen pond and threatening snow for later in the day. Grammie's breath turned into little puffs of frost as she chucked Molly's tennis ball ahead. Molly ran full out, not noticing or caring about anything beyond the yellow, fuzz-coated missile she chased.

I could feel William's presence growing stronger with each step closer to the pond, so much so that my vision blurred with anticipation when I reached its edge. A solid layer of ice coated the pond, thick and strong enough for Grammie to walk on top of it. With a deep breath, she muttered a prayer for courage, stepped out onto the expanse of silvery gray, and we started making our way toward its center.

"Should have brought skates."

"I don't think I own any skates. " If I did, they were probably hanging in Dad's workshop somewhere. Or else Catherine might have a pair floating around the old house, but if she did, I hadn't seen them yet, nor did I have time for fruitless searching. Plus, ice skates on my feet, even when I wasn't in my own body, were likely to lead to the necessity of crutches. I didn't need that angst in my life.

A darker bank of clouds swallowed up the sun, so all that remained was an eerie silence broken only by the sound of my grandmother's hesitant footsteps and my dog's breathing. I closed my eyes and focused on William's energy, trying to sense where he was. Suddenly, a loud cracking noise filled the air, and Grammie let out a yelp.

"It's okay," I said, trying to sound more confident than I felt. "Just the ice shifting. This pond isn't that deep, but maybe it's better if you take Molly back to the car."

"But I want to see the ghost," Grammie argued. "I don't want to be stuck in the car while you have all the fun."

Molly tugged at her leash, anxious to get off the cracking ice. Grammie took one last look around before leading the dog back to the pond's edge, where it was shallow enough to keep Molly safe while I continued searching for William. The clouds had grown darker, and the temperature had dropped significantly since we'd arrived, but there was something else. A spark of what I assumed to be William's presence, so I stood in the middle of the pond calling his name.

"I've talked to Victoria," I offered as bait. "She misses her husband and wants nothing more than to be reunited with the love of her life. Don't you want that, too? I'm here to help."

I babbled similar nonsense for about ten minutes before finally concluding that William didn't want to talk to me.

The first flakes of snow tickled across the ice as I made my way back to the shore.

"You didn't miss anything. Any idea why he wouldn't engage at all?"

"Not off the top of my head. Did you feel him?"

Shrugging, I went with the truth. "I think so. I felt something, and we've been told he should be there, so I might have imagined feeling his presence."

"Maybe you're still blocked."

"From when you hypnotized me? Wouldn't that have ended when I...became disembodied?"

Her turn to shrug. "I don't know all the ins and outs of life, death, or hypnotism. Your grandfather was big on the how-to, less so on the why and why not of things."

We rode in silence for a mile or so while I considered the possibility. "I didn't have any trouble seeing Abner." The conversation dropped while she stopped to fill the car's tank with gas, and I had to talk her through using my debit card because she'd never consented to get one of her own. No amount of explanation had bridged the difference between a debit card and a credit card in her eyes.

Back on the road, she drove through a curtain of falling snow as she picked things up where we'd left off.

"Abner was an active haunter. You didn't have to work hard to see him because he was the one making all the effort. He wanted to be seen and showed himself. That's the difference."

"Yes," I admitted. "That fits with my experience. To a point, I suppose."

"But I think I need to remove the block anyway."

"Can you hypnotize me if I'm…like this," I gestured to my ghostly body.

She shrugged and pulled into the grocery store parking lot. "Only one way to find out. We'll try it tonight. Does Drew like dynamites?"

"Drew likes everything."

"Good. I'll cook up a batch for him. If he's anything like me, he'll want comfort food on a nasty night. This storm's going to dump at least six inches on us. I can feel it in my bones."

With predictions for just that, I figured she wasn't wrong and gave her additional points for navigating the grocery store without running into anyone who knew me well enough to chat, except for Robin Thackery.

"That girl's not right in the head," Grammie said when we got back to the car after she'd watched Robin drop two heavy cans of tomato sauce on top of the bag containing four green peppers.

"You caught her on a good day."

The mix of dread and anticipation is a particularly annoying cocktail. Especially when you're incorporeal and have no physical outlet for the anxiety rolling around in your gut. Grammie didn't seem to feel any of the weight I did as she tossed ground beef into a cast iron dutch oven warming over high heat. While the hamburger browned, she cut green peppers, onions, and celery into large chunks and opened cans of tomatoes—chopped, sauce, and paste. "Watching you cook brings back memories."

"Your mother adds garlic."

"Yes, I know," I said. This was a long-standing point of disagreement between them. I'd always been on Grammie's side of that one. "I don't, but I do put nuts in my brownies." Another bone of contention, but one where I sided with my mother. "The more nuts, the better. And no frosting."

With a final flourish, she dumped the last of the vegetables into the steaming pot and turned the burner down to let it simmer. We talked about our next steps with William until Drew got home, then after they ate, got down to the business of hypnotizing me.

"Are you comfortable?"

"Comfortable as a ghost can get." Not for lack of trying, I hadn't managed to muster enough energy to touch anything in the physical world, which meant I hovered over the bed rather than lying on it. Not exactly comfortable, but not uncomfortable. Mostly, I just felt profoundly disconnected from everything.

"Okay. Now, I want you to focus on your breathing. Take a deep breath in, and let it out slowly."

I tried. You have to give me credit for that much.

"Um, you know I'm on the other side of the veil and don't have a body. How am I supposed to focus on my breathing when I can't breathe?"

You also have to give my grandmother credit for not

having a fragile ego. When confronted with the absurdity of what she'd asked me to do, she saw the humor and began to laugh. Which set me off, so I joined in. Soon, she was the one who needed to focus on her breathing because laughter had stolen most of it from her.

"Is everything okay in there?" Drew yelled from the kitchen.

"We're fine, but that's not going to work. Let's try another way."

Rising, she moved across to the dresser, opened my jewelry box, and pulled out a pendant watch she'd worn during my childhood. "You kept this old thing?"

"Why wouldn't I? It reminds me of you." I reached out to stroke the watch, but my finger went right through.

"Good." Grammie Dupree settled back in her former position and dangled the watch in front of my face. "Watch the watch. Focus on it, and only it. If anything else, any other thought pops into your head, don't get distracted. Just let it slide right back out without giving it any of your attention."

While she spoke in an even tone, she kept the watch moving. "Are you sure this will work? It seems like something out of a Saturday morning cartoon."

"Don't make fun of the process," she chided. "You need to find a focal point so you can get into a fully-relaxed state. It could have been anything. A pendant, a crystal, a fishing bobber. Heck, your grandfather once hypnotized a cow with a tea ball so she would stand still and let the vet turn a breech calf."

"I didn't know farm animals were susceptible."

157

"Maybe not, but it worked that time." With a practiced flick of her wrist, the watch began to swing again. "Focus and relax. Relax and focus." Her voice took on the rhythm of the watch, like a metronome, keeping the beat until I felt everything settle.

"You feel calm, rested, and relaxed as the sound of my voice takes you deeper and deeper."

My eyes flickered closed as the warmth and comfort of her voice took me under. Colors danced before my eyes. Reds, yellows, greens, and blues. A rainbow of gently pulsating light that expanded to envelop me in and pull me out of myself.

She was right. I did feel calm, rested, and relaxed. Probably for the first time in weeks—certainly the first time since the body-switching debacle. It felt so good I could have stayed in that state forever. As agreed, and with little fuss, she removed the mental block she'd installed in my head.

"I will count down from ten to zero. As I do, your full awareness will return. You will awaken feeling refreshed and ready to take on the day."

Ghosts don't sleep, or maybe it's more accurate to say *disembodied spirits don't sleep*, but coming back to myself did feel a bit like awakening, and I did feel refreshed.

"Did it work?" I sat up straight.

"How should I know?"

It occurred to me that we might not have thought through all the implications or possibilities, but at this point, it didn't matter. "I guess we'll find out the next time we run into a ghost. I'm not sure what to expect."

"Me, either."

158

With the day's work done, she and Drew settled into their nightly routine where Grammie watched TV in the living room, and Drew either went up to his room or downstairs to play video games in his man cave. Tonight, he'd chosen the basement and the companionship of a white dragon. And me. Not that I was much of a companion.

I didn't understand the rules but enjoyed watching his character storm the castle, and when he paused to get a snack, I stayed behind while he went upstairs. He returned with a bag of microwave popcorn in his hand and a weird expression on his face.

"Everly! Are you still here?" Waiting for me to declare my presence, Drew stood in awkward silence. I tapped him on the arm to put him out of his misery.

"Oh, good. Listen, we have to do something about your grandmother."

He paused as if waiting for me to ask why, then realized I couldn't and continued. "She turned Project Runway into a drinking game."

I tapped his arm three times. A new signal he interpreted correctly as me needing more information.

"Yeah. She thought it would be fun to take a drink whenever anyone said they knew who they were as a designer, and now, she's hammered."

It was too late to do anything about it other than pour her into bed if she didn't make it there on her own.

"Then again, she's an adult, I suppose. It might be best if I let her sort herself out."

That got a single tap from me. This situation wasn't easy on me, and for all her breezy self-assurance that everything would turn out okay, Grammie Dupree had to be worried, too. If my memories were accurate, she hadn't been the type of person to overindulge with alcohol regularly, so at this point, I wasn't too worried about her.

With the concern gone from his face, Drew kicked off his shoes and settled on the sofa, leaning back against a throw pillow with his hands behind his head and his legs propped on a footstool, crossed at the ankles. He made a fine picture. Too bad I couldn't touch him.

"She's a hell of a woman," he finally said, and since I agreed with him, he got a tap on the knee. "But then, so is your mother. You're a credit to them both." He got another tap, but only for the comments about them.

When he sat up suddenly, swung his legs to the floor, rested his elbows on his knees and his head in his hands, my heart wrenched. Maybe he'd hit the end of the line on the crazy train that my life had become. I couldn't blame him if he had. A girlfriend who sees ghosts is one thing, but when she turns into one, that's a lot to take. If he were sensible, there'd be a Drew-shaped hole in the wall as he escaped.

"Come back to me, okay? I miss you."

"I will," I said, but he didn't hear me.

Chapter 20

Grammie's prediction of six inches of snow was off by a couple. Mooselick River endured an eight-inch coating of fluffy white before the last flake fell. Kids got a day off school, and so did my dad, so when he showed up at my front door a couple of hours before lunch, he met Drew on his way to work.

"Don't forget," Drew locked eyes with my grandmother and did the two finger pointing thing from his face to hers.

"I gave my word, didn't I?"

"What's that all about?" Dad wanted to know. So did I.

"Oh, just something he asked me to do later. Nothing to worry about."

Once Drew was gone, Dad hugged his mother, then addressed the empty space about five feet from where I stood.

"I've got something to show you. You'll both want to see this." He sniffed the air and pulled a laptop out of the bag he carried that I hadn't noticed. "Got any more of that coffee I smell?"

"Mom doesn't let him have coffee after noon," I said.

"Won't you get into trouble with Kitty?"

"Not if you don't tell her," Dad grinned. He would miss his mother when she left, but this had to be as weird for him as it was for me. She mimed turning a key over her lips and followed him to the kitchen, where he set the computer down and flipped open the top. "What's your Wi-Fi password?"

"Sunbeambagel606," I gave it to Grammie to relay to him, which she did, but with an amused expression.

"Who comes up with such silliness?" Grammie said as she poured a cup from the pot Drew had left running.

Once he'd logged on, Dad navigated to the website with the webcam feed and logged into that as well. With a practiced hand, he chose the history link and selected the hour he wanted to view. Then, when the still of the town came up, he clicked on it to start the video.

All I saw was a steady curtain of snow and several humps around a larger one, which I assumed with the Nativity scene.

"That's from last night. We got the cameras up and running before the storm hit. I was checking the footage to see if we had any trouble with the wind shaking the mount because it got pretty breezy around two in the morning, and take a look at this."

He'd begun to fast forward while he talked, stopped at the appropriate timestamp, then hit play again. "Do you see it?"

At first, I didn't, but Grammie, standing to his right, clamped a hand on his shoulder and leaned closer to the screen. "Just call me a monkey's uncle," she said, and he kicked the speed down to go frame by frame.

On the screen, what looked like a ghostly, glowing figure of a woman with long hair and wearing a pair of overalls and a flannel shirt was slowly walking across the square, carrying three plastic flamingos in her arms.

"That's Lily Evergreen," Grammie said. "Isn't it?"

Dad nodded and smiled. "Looks like her to me, too. She and her brother ran the Christmas tree farm after their parents retired. Her nephew owns it now. He's expanded the place quite a bit." He pointed at the screen again. "Look, she's adding those plastic birds to the Nativity scene."

I leaned closer and saw that she was indeed placing them in a line near the left of the screen. So much for Martha's theory of kids having fun with the display.

"What do you think? Does that beat the time we put Principal Deacon's lawn furniture on his roof?" Dad said to Grammie.

"I didn't know you could see ghosts," she sounded miffed.

"I can't. Not in real life."

"There's a lot of ghost footage online, but this is different. Look at the clarity." Grammie repeated my comment so my father could hear it. "I bet that's because she ramped up her energy to move the flamingos."

We watched as Lily finished arranging the bits of pink plastic and then vanished into thin air without leaving so much as a swirl of snowflakes in her wake. It was eerie.

"Wow," I said softly as Dad paused the video and returned to the list of times to select the next one.

"I'll make some changes to the settings, but for now, we're recording and saving in one-hour increments. She comes back in the next one, too. She's only there at the beginning, and then the line of flamingos takes her out of range. Do you want to see?"

After we'd scanned through the rest and watched Lily place the silly birds in a line leading out of the frame, he closed out the window on his laptop and shut it down. Despite the cozy warmth of the kitchen, he shivered, and I realized I'd stood too close, so I stepped back.

Eyelids drooping shut, Grammie tipped her head back slightly and took a moment to think. "What I remember of her, which isn't much, Lily was a sweet girl. Gentle-natured. Tender."

"That's my recollection as well," Dad said. "We didn't run in the same circles."

"Do you think she's trying to tell us something?"

Dad shrugged when she relayed my question, but Grammie's eyes lit up. "Maybe she's trying to lead us to something. You know, like a treasure hunt!"

I raised an eyebrow. "A treasure hunt?"

She nodded eagerly and clapped her hands together in excitement. "Why not? She made a line of flamingos, didn't she? We could follow it and see where they lead us. It'll be an adventure."

Dad chuckled. "I think you've been watching too many movies, Mom."

But I was intrigued, and we had nothing better to do until later in the day. Mooselick River was enjoying its first snow day of the season, and the idea of solving a minor mystery appealed. "Why not? It could be fun." And we might learn something about Lily in the process. Even if everything went well with the Weeping Widow, and I didn't need Lily as a backup for returning to normal, I would offer my help if she wanted to cross over.

Grammie clapped her hands together. "Excellent! I'll put on a coat, and we can start at the Nativity scene. Who knows where we'll end up? It's not every day I get to play in the snow with my favorite people in the world."

As she bustled off to the bedroom, I sat with my dad. Despite the strange circumstances, it was nice to spend time with him, and Grammie always knew how to make things interesting. Once she got herself all bundled up, we made our way into the center of town and then through the snow-covered streets, following the trail of plastic flamingos that Lily had left behind.

We weren't the only ones, either. With school out for the day, a couple of kids also followed the bright pink figures through the snow. Those few hardy souls who weren't bothered by the storm's aftermath craned their necks to see what was happening as they drove past, but nobody stopped. It was like we were all caught up in some kind of dream.

The trail of flamingos led us around the gazebo, across the street, and through the parking lot, where mounds of snow marked the beginnings of several large sculptures for the lighting festival.

"Lame," one of our young entourage declared, and when he turned back, the rest followed, leaving the three of us alone.

"Where do you think these all came from?" Dad wondered. "There must have been fifty of them. I don't know anyone who has fifty plastic flamingos just lying around."

"I do," I said. "She got them from the storage building at the town office."

165

When Grammie repeated what I'd said, Dad snapped his fingers. "That's right. They'd be left over from the luau debacle of two…no, three years ago."

"Do tell."

I hadn't heard this one before, either.

"All I'll say is that it takes twice as long to roast a whole pig as Martha thought, and dollar store flamingos are too small to make effective signposts. People didn't see them, and they didn't show up in droves to eat the mostly-raw pig that didn't finish cooking until breakfast time on Sunday."

Poor Martha, I thought. Even if she fell here and there, at least she'd had the guts to try and bring the town back from the dead when no one else seemed to care. I felt bad for her, though, if people still talked about her mistakes this many years later.

"Still, it wasn't all bad. Do you know what happened the next morning?"

Grammie shook her head. So did I.

"Half the town showed up with grills, camp stoves, and frying pans. The grocery store donated some stuff, and we had a pork and egg community breakfast that no one will ever forget. It did bring everyone together for a day, so I guess I wouldn't call it a debacle. At least she tried."

"Do you think this is what Lily was trying to show us?" I gestured toward the mound of snow, waiting for the sculptor to make it into something else. "I mean, I'm not sure I see the point."

Grammie shrugged. "I don't get it, either." She eyed the pile that was twice as tall as her. "Should we come back with shovels?"

"We can't. For one thing, it would take more than the two of you to move that mountain, and the festival is tomorrow, so we really shouldn't."

"I'd rather not." Dad stepped forward and brushed at the snow near the last flamingo. Finding nothing, he straightened and shrugged. Then he tilted his head and wrinkled his forehead. "But look over there."

Over there was another flamingo. The first in a second line leading out of the parking lot, across several front lawns, and ending with us having to climb the fence to get into the cemetery. I'd never trespassed so many times in a single week.

The last flamingo leaned against a headstone. The first one to reach it, Dad used his gloved hand to swipe drifted white away from the gray granite.

"It says, 'Abigail Winters'."

Dad trailed off, squinting at the inscription. "I know that name."

Her eyes narrowing as she studied the inscription, Grammie said, "I know it, too." She leaned in closer, brushing away more of the snow. "Beloved daughter and friend. I'd forgotten all about Abigail. Such a tragic story."

"Abigail Winters?" I repeated, feeling a chill run down my spine. "Who was she?"

Grammie turned to me, a serious expression on her face. "Abigail Winters and her family lived out near Lily's family's place. She died young."

"I can see that by the dates on the headstone. She didn't even graduate high school. What happened to her?"

Dad nodded. "I remember Abby. She and Lily were as

tight as a glued-up joint." Leave it to my dad to use a woodworking reference. "Lily took it hard when Abby was killed. I don't think she was ever the same afterward."

"Tell me."

"Two girls walked home from the school bus drop-off. One made it; the other didn't," Grammie said and crossed herself. "Put the whole town on edge until they arrested the killer. Took long enough, but they didn't have as much of the crime-solving hocus pocus as there is now."

"It wasn't that long ago," Dad hunkered down to wipe more snow from around the headstone. "The eighties weren't the dark ages."

"That must have been hard on Lily. I'm betting they looked at her?" Again, my question had to be relayed. This ghost business was frustrating.

Dad nodded and said, "For a minute, but there was a crew running at the farm, getting ready to plant. Six guys hired on from town. They all saw Lily come home, and Abigail kept walking. Lily went inside, came out a little while later to help with the planting, and was in plain sight of plenty of witnesses at the time of the murder."

"You know Ernie Polk's uncle Avery was just about the worst officer of the law in the history of this town. Scared that girl half to death, he did. I know because I happened to stop in at the grocery store when her mother caught up with Avery and gave him a piece of her mind right there in the parking lot. She had plenty to say and didn't much care who heard it."

Turning away from the headstone, Grammie began to

make her way out of the cemetery with her son trailing behind. "They found that poor girl's body not even a hundred feet from the road. She'd been strangled, and it was clear as day Lily didn't have anything to do with it."

Dad passed us, unlocked the car doors, and held the door for her. The windshield had frosted over while we were gone, so he turned on the heat and picked up the conversation where we'd left off. "It was, but that didn't matter. You know I love living where you can knock on your neighbor's door if you need help, but there's that other side of small-town life where people are happy to paint their neighbors with a guilty brush just for the sake of drama."

That was not news to me, but I could attest from personal experience that small towns weren't the only places where idle gossip could turn to barbed weapons aimed at someone's reputation. Lily had been the focus of speculation, and I knew exactly how she'd felt. It made me want to help her even more.

"But you said they solved the case, right? Who killed Abigail, then? Someone from town?"

"Everly wants to know whodunit," Grammie explained, then continued, "Some boy she'd been seeing from Bangor. Her parents didn't approve of him."

"For good reason."

The windows finally clear, Dad pulled onto the road and circled the block to turn around, which took us back past the cemetery. I looked over at the grave, feeling a sense of unease. "Do you think Lily was trying to tell us something about Abigail's death? Maybe there was more to it than what the police found out."

Grammie shrugged. "It's possible. We won't know

until we start digging."

"Digging?" I repeated, feeling a pang of anxiety. "You mean, like, digging up the grave?"

"No." She swiveled in her seat and looked at me like I was stupid. "What on earth would we do that for?" She shuddered at the thought. "It's winter, the ground is frozen, and digging up the dead isn't strictly legal. I meant on your computer. You know, research, like we did for Victoria."

"Victoria?" Dad had only heard half the conversation. "Who's Victoria?"

"You've heard of the Weeping Widow," Grammie told him, and when he nodded, she continued, "Well, we're reuniting her with her lost husband in the hope that I can tag along when she crosses over."

The drive home passed quickly while she told him what we'd learned and what we planned to do about it.

Back in my driveway, he let the car idle while he asked, "When?"

"Soon as it gets dark."

To give mother and son a few minutes alone, I drifted toward the house, coming up short when the tether that held me to my body snapped taut. Since that tether was the only thing giving me hope that getting back into my body was possible, I didn't test its strength and moved back enough to give it some slack and waited near the front steps. If our plan worked, this would be Dad's chance to say goodbye, and judging from the way she stroked his cheek and he rested his forehead against hers, they were taking that bittersweet moment now.

When they broke apart, and my grandmother glanced around to see where I'd gone, I waved to show I was fine. Dad's face was as solemn as it had been on the day we'd first lost Grammie Dupree, but underneath the solemn, I sensed a new peace. Not that there'd been anything left unsaid between mother and son, but she hadn't known who any of us were for most of the last year of her life. This bizarre interlude had given them a do-over. A deathly do-over.

That would make a great book title, I thought.

Chapter 21

"Why is it taking so long?" Grammie's stomach grumbled loudly enough for me to hear it from several feet away.

My computer had popped up with an update when we turned it on to begin our search for Abigail Winters. Half an hour later, we were still looking at the spinning circle of annoyance.

"I don't know. It's just one of life's many frustrations. Why don't you go grab something to eat? I thought I just heard your stomach singing the blues."

"It's trying to eat my backbone, so I'll do that." She buzzed around the kitchen, getting herself a sandwich and some soup. Grilled cheese cut into triangles just the way she'd always done, and tomato soup for comfort. A flood of love and memories rose up to swamp over me. I'd missed her so much. This time with her was a blessing, but blessings wouldn't be enough to fill the hole she'd leave when she went back into the light.

We chatted about other things while she ate. Stories of my dad's childhood mostly. Some I'd heard before, and others that were new to me. The update finished while she put her dishes into the dishwasher.

"You're getting better at this," I said when she

grabbed the mouse, navigated to the browser, and typed in Abigail's name.

Keeping my distance, I leaned over her shoulder, eagerly reading the results that scrolled down the screen.

"There's an article from the Bangor Daily." She clicked and began to murmur the finer points as we read them. "Pretty girl." There'd been a photo attached to the article. "Well-liked. Outgoing. Starred in the school play two years running and sang in the chorus and the church choir. Not the type to date a lowlife murderer."

A mugshot of the killer popped up as we scrolled down. "No. But does he look like a lowlife murderer to you?"

She shrugged. "Can't go by looks. You put trash in a gift bag, it's still trash."

"So I've heard."

"But I'm not seeing the big mystery here." Shoving fingers through unruly curls, Grammie scratched her scalp. "It makes my head itch just trying to see how any of this makes a difference for Lily. What was she trying to tell us?"

"I'm not sure. Keep reading, and remember, we still have a few lines to tug. Lily was related to the Evergreens that own the tree farm, meaning she has to be Chris Evergreen's aunt, cousin, or something. Chris is a friend of mine, and also, he's Patrea's husband," Everly explained. "I really should have made the connection when her name first came up. It's not that common a name."

"I knew the family. Good, solid, hardworking people. If this Chris is anything like his father, your friend did well for herself."

"She did, but then, so did he. Patrea comes off a bit prickly sometimes, but she has a lot of heart. Still, she didn't think she was cut out for a long-term relationship, and Chris wasn't looking for it either. But they met, and there were so many sparks they ended up getting married last summer. Just between you and me, they're already thinking about starting a family."

After I gave her the highlights of Patrea's Christmas romance, we moved on to the next article from the search results.

One fateful afternoon in 1981, Abigail and Lily walked home after the school bus dropped them at the end of their road. The two girls were seen by several passersby, enjoying the late spring weather and talking animatedly. Lily went inside when she got to her place, and Abigail continued on but never made it home. The entire town was shocked, and, by all accounts, Lily was devastated.

"The more I read, the more it all comes back to me." Leaving a smear on the screen, Grammie tapped it with her finger. "Lily Evergreen swore on her own mother's life that Abigail had been fine and happy when they parted ways. When the short investigation ended, Abigail's parents moved away, but Lily was never the same. Instead of going off to college when she graduated, Lily took up residence in a small cottage on the Evergreen's farm and continued working there."

"That's sad. She never got married? Had a family?" I hoped she'd found some happiness after her great loss.

"Not that I ever heard, but let's see." Like a pro, Grammie opened another browser tab and typed in Lily's name, then clicked on the link to her obituary.

"Looks like only blood family listed among her survivors. No husband, no kids."

"That's sad, and it doesn't say how she died, either. Click the back button and see what else we can find. Martha mentioned her that day she discovered the missing donkey." I began to pace. "Do you remember? She said something about Lily's tragic passing and how they hadn't used the Nativity scene since. Don't you think that's odd?"

"I do not," Grammie turned from the screen, her eyes gleaming. "Because Lily died at this time of year, and it says here her body was found in the Nativity scene."

Getting too close, I leaned in again to read and jumped back when she flinched. Whenever I went into the light, and I hoped that wouldn't be for a very long time, I'd have to hunt down Amber and apologize for thinking she lacked respect for my personal space during her time with me. Turns out, it's easier to brush up against the living than I thought.

"How did she die? Does it say?"

"Fell off the roof while adjusting the Star of David. According to this, the fall didn't kill her immediately. She crawled inside, and they found her the next day. The official cause of death was hypothermia. Is that a fancy word for freezing to death?"

"It is. No wonder they stopped using the Nativity scene. I wonder how her family feels now that it's out again."

"If I'd known that, I would've let Martha put up her stupid white trees."

"Of course, you would have. But this does explain some things. No wonder Martha looked so funny. She

175

must have thought I knew Lily's story, but I don't remember anything about it."

Puzzled, I moved back toward the computer so I could see the dates. "Oh. That explains it. I was in college then and had already met Paul. Mom was barely speaking to me at the time. She wouldn't have called for anything short of a personal tragedy, and this wasn't one of those."

We'd had a few rocky spots, my mother and me, and Lily had died during the absolute worst of them. I hadn't been in touch with anyone from back home, and I hadn't been close friends with Chris at the time, so I hadn't heard the story.

Chapter 22

"We don't have to do this now," I said as we pulled into the same parking spot at Shady Acres from the day before and looked at the expanse of unbroken snow between us and the pond. "It was one thing yesterday with all that hard crust to walk on, but that's a solid quarter of a mile hike, right there."

"You need to be back in your own skin by Christmas, and that skin isn't made of cotton candy. I won't melt."

But she would sink to her knees and struggle for maybe half a dozen steps before giving up. I'd have quit at two.

"You win," she said. "I'm going back to the car. Don't be all day, okay? Check for the ghost and then come back."

"I don't have to check for him. I can see from here. He's standing at the center of the pond watching us."

"You're killing me here. You know that? I can't see him, so I guess it's a good thing I've decided to go sit in the car." Pulling off a huffy exit isn't as easy as you might think when it requires wallowing through deep snow. Still, Grammie gave it her best effort and pulled it off nicely.

With the implications of her not seeing William

running through my head, I set off across the white surface, feeling thankful for the ghostly perk of not sinking. William waited and watched as I made my way closer.

"Mr. Eastman?"

He nodded. "Yes, that's me." I could see why Victoria waited for him. William Eastman had been a fine-looking man with kind eyes of the warmest brown. At the moment, those eyes held a great deal of confusion.

"I've been looking for you," I said, my voice barely above a whisper.

"Then I suppose it's a good thing you found me, for I've not the faintest idea where I am."

Couldn't he see the assisted living facility a few hundred yards away?

"What happened to you? What do you remember about how you came to be here? Did you see the person who attacked you?"

"Attacked?" William frowned and sighed. "I went out fishing and got turned around. I'm not sure why I left the river. I just remember feeling one of my funny spells coming on, and then I was here. I don't know where I am, and I can't seem to find my way home. Can you help me? Do you know my wife? Her name is Victoria."

"I've met Victoria. She's waiting for you. I can take her to you if you'd like." I looked at William, my curiosity growing. "But what do you mean by *funny spell*?" I asked. "Would you mind walking with me?" I figured if Grammie couldn't come to the ghost, I'd bring the ghost to her.

William paused for a moment before speaking, but he

178

followed me back toward the parking lot. His voice was hesitant as if he was trying to figure out how to explain what had happened. "It's nothing," he said. "I don't remember anything." He paused again, his eyes distant as he remembered the experience. "Did you say you could help me get home?"

I had said so and would, of course, follow through on that promise, but curiosity wouldn't let me just take him to Victoria without learning more about him.

"I mean you no harm, William. Please accept my solemn promise that I don't. I'd like to hear more about what happened to you while I take you to see your wife. Is that okay?"

Did he even know he was dead? I wondered, and my next thought followed through on the same lines. Would I have to explain that to him, and if so, what should I say?

"I so did not ask for this job," I muttered.

"Job?" William glanced sideways at me but fell into step like I'd hoped he would.

"Never mind. Tell me everything you remember since you left the river. Did you see your attacker?"

"There was no," William stopped, and so did I. He put his hand to the back of his head. "Yes, the attacker." Something about the way he'd stopped and changed tack made me suspicious, but I said nothing as he continued. "I remember the fish were biting well, and I'd caught two already but wanted to try for a third when the attacker struck." He rubbed his forehead as if the memory of it still caused him pain.

I watched him carefully, trying to piece together the facts because while William Eastman might be a good

179

provider and the kind of man a woman would wait an eternity for, he was also a liar.

"I remember my head hurt, and there was this buzzing sound in my ears. Then, I was here." He stopped again, turned, and pointed. "Or there. I tried to find my way home, but every path circled back to this place, so I stayed."

"For a long time." The words popped out before I could bite them back.

"A very long time." At least he confirmed he'd been aware of the passage of time. Maybe he did know he was dead. I supposed I could ask him, but if I did, and if he freaked out the way murdered ghosts do, I'd not only lose my chance to get him to cross over today but would have to get Grammie to trek back out here, however many times it took to build back William's trust.

No, it was now or never, and if I ended up back in my body with my curiosity unsatisfied, that was a price I was willing to pay.

"Did you have enemies? You must know who would have wanted to kill you."

"My mother threatened to send me to the great beyond a time or two when I got underfoot, but I can't think of another soul who would want to do me in." He tried. I could see the concentration on his face while he considered. In my experience, murdered ghosts want justice so they can move on. They want it enough they become fixated and hound me to find peace for them. William didn't seem that bothered. What's more, considering his death didn't seem to shake up his presence in the way it had for the ghosts I'd encountered in the past. Maybe he wasn't murdered after all.

Carefully, I prodded. "Did you hear or see anyone nearby while fishing that day?"

"Not a single soul."

We weren't getting anywhere like this. I needed to push him harder; if he poofed, we'd just have to deal with it.

"Think harder, William. It's of vital importance."

"Why?" He wanted to know. "Why can't you just take me back to the river? I can find my way home from there. I just want to go home."

Because I could, I put a hand on his arm for comfort. "I'm sorry. I know this isn't easy. I've helped a few people in your situation, and finding out what happened to them is always the key, but there's no reason why we can't talk about it on the way back to the river."

William's face lit with joy. "You'll take me home?"

"Count on it. Follow me." Turning, I headed back to the car. "It's a short drive. We'll have you home in no time."

When no response came, I turned back to see William lying in the snow, his body shaking uncontrollably. "What happened?" Running back, I dropped to my knees, thankful the cold and wet didn't soak through my pants. I guess being on this side of the veil came with a few perks.

After a moment, William came back to himself and tried to scramble up.

"Just sit still for a minute," I ordered as my mind got busy considering the implications of what I'd just seen. "Was that what you meant before when you said you felt funny?"

William nodded. "Just a flutter this time."

181

"And on the day you got lost, it was more than a flutter?"

While he rested, William recounted his memory of those final moments. As I listened to him recount his story, a realization began to dawn on me: William hadn't been murdered at all. It was more likely he experienced a seizure while out fishing all those years ago. Or a series of them. He'd become disoriented, walked in the wrong direction, and during a final grand mal, had repeatedly bashed his head on a rock. Between the head injury and exposure, William had died alone and not a mile from his house as the crow flies.

"That must have been terrifying and lonely," I said softly, looking him in the eye with sympathy and understanding as I offered a hand to help him up.

William nodded solemnly. "I've been alone and lost for a very long time. I know it's time to cross into the light, but I can't until I find my way home."

I nodded, feeling a surge of determination in my heart. "I've spoken to Victoria. She's waiting for you."

William's eyes lit up with hope. "You have? She is?"

"Yes," I said firmly. "Come on. Let's go."

With that, we set off, walking across the frozen pond and toward the parking lot where Grammie still waited.

"I don't know how to ride in the red machine." William eyed the SUV with trepidation.

"But you have seen cars before, right?" He'd been close enough to Shady Acres to have seen a lot of things. "It's easy. You just sort of slide right through the door and imagine yourself sitting on the seat. Don't think about it too hard, or you'll fall through. Like this." I showed him, and after a couple of tries, he managed to get himself inside the car.

"Good to meet you, young fellow," Grammie spun to offer him a smile.

"You can see him, then?" Despite a lifetime of believing in the spirit world, Grammie Dupree couldn't actually see most ghosts. Now that she was in my body and had removed her post-hypnotic suggestion, we would learn if that ability was tied to my physical body.

"Clear as day."

"Ma'am." William tipped his hat, then let go of it and grabbed for the back of the seat when she put the car in gear and hit the gas to back out of the space. "Jesus, Mary, and Joseph," he muttered.

"They can't help you," Grammie tossed over her shoulder, "Besides, you're already dead. What's the worst that can happen to you if I wreck the car? You ain't getting any deader."

"I suppose that's true." But William didn't relax, and neither did I until we turned down a dirt road and drove slowly, watching for the spot where the snowmobile trail crossed. If we'd plotted correctly, this crossing would allow for the closest access to the spot where I'd found Victoria.

"There," I saw the sign in the distance. "And it looks like there's been snowmobile traffic already, so you'll have the packed-down trail to walk most of the way."

"Good thing." In the falling darkness, Grammie eyed the snowshoes we'd stuffed into the back seat with disgust, but she'd have to wear them for a short distance once we left the trail. With snowshoes, it's all about getting the rhythm right. I never minded using them, but she'd been dreading them ever since we left the house.

Grammie flicked on the flashlight Drew had chosen for its wide beam. He'd also packed a headlamp, a day's worth of rations, waterproof matches, a knife, rope, first aid supplies, and one of those blankets that look like they're made from aluminum foil. She'd texted him when we left the car, and he'd made her promise to text him every twenty minutes until we got back to it.

"Did he give you a compass and a flare gun, too?"

"Probably. You want me to look?"

"No, and you'll be fine with the snowshoes. And don't forget, if we do this right, you only have to worry about getting there. This will be a one-way trip for you."

"What does that mean?" William's energy grew brighter as the sound of babbling stream waters grew louder.

"Nothing," I said, then curiosity kicked in. "What do you see when you look at us?"

"A young woman wearing a somewhat immodest jumper and an older woman with laughing eyes."

He saw souls and not bodies, but there wasn't time to tell him our story since we'd come to the spot nearest the stream.

"This is it. Are you ready?" I was asking Grammie, but William answered with a firm affirmative. "Then let's do this."

"One minute." Her lips twisted into a wry smile, she rummaged through the backpack and came up with a length of neon orange plastic, which she tied to the branches of the tree nearest to where we left the trail. "Drew said I had to."

"He really loves us."

It took nearly as long to walk the hundred feet or so to

the riverbank as it had to hike the half mile of snowmobile trail. Snowshoes are fine on flat ground but can be less easy to maneuver going up or downhill. Still, Grammie managed it with her normal fiery aplomb.

"It's just around this corner, William."

We arrived at her favorite spot to find Victoria, the weeping widow, standing in a pool of moonlight. She was a beautiful sight, with her pale skin and long white dress, her eyes shining with tears.

William rushed over to her, and they embraced tightly. Victoria's tears flowed freely down her cheeks as they held each other closely. "Oh, William," she sobbed into his shoulder. "Where have you been all this time?"

He took her face in his hands and kissed away her tears. "I'm so sorry, my love," he said softly. "I got lost for a while. A long while, it seems. I've missed you."

Victoria nodded slowly before looking up at me with gratitude. "Thank you for bringing him back to me," she said sincerely before turning back to William with a smile on her face. "It's time for us to go home now."

"It was my pleasure," I said, tears in my eyes.

Victoria smiled at me, then looked back at William. "Come, my love. I've quite an adventure and many tales to tell. Wait until you hear about the red driving machine."

As the couple turned to walk into the intense light that had begun to shine, Grammie grabbed onto me and rushed forward. "This is it," she looked back at me, her face falling into shadow as she said goodbye. "Darling girl, I love—"

One snowshoe fouled against the other, and she went

down so quickly that she dragged my astral body under the snow.

"No," Grammie shouted. "William, wait. Victoria, please." But they were gone. The light dimmed to darkness without her in it. When she let loose with language hot enough to melt snow, I joined her. Then we texted Drew the bad news and began the trek back to the road.

"If I hadn't had those stupid beavertails on," Grammie repeated the half-sentence several times along the way. But it didn't matter now. We'd lost our chance. "Good thing Lily Evergreen's still hanging around."

"She's our last chance."

Nothing like jumping right into the pressure cooker and turning up the heat.

Chapter 23

The Friday morning drive to the library passed with very little conversation since we were both still smarting from the epic failure of the night before. Warmer overnight temperatures slimmed inches off snowbanks, turning parking lots into sloppy slush pools.

"I see you're still here." If my mother meant that to come out sounding nice, she missed the mark by a mile.

"It's not her fault, Mom. Things moved pretty fast once Victoria and William got a look at each other. In retrospect, I guess we should have given one or both of them a heads-up so they'd help. That was our mistake and one I don't intend to make with Lily Evergreen."

Mom lifted her eyebrows, "Your father showed me the video. I still find it hard to believe. Don't you think I'd have run into her if she was still hanging around?"

"Well, she is." I cut off whatever nasty comment my grandmother began to make. "That's why we're here. We've done some research online, but I guess I was in college when Lily passed, so I didn't hear about her death, and the news article we found didn't give much detail. We were hoping you'd have more information. We're running out of ghosts, so getting this one right is imperative."

"If you promise to let me be more involved this time, I'll tell you everything I know about the death of Lily Evergreen," Kitty said softly and waited for us to agree. "You probably already have the broad strokes. Lily fell while adding a star to the roof of the Nativity scene. Some kids found her body next to the manger on their way to school the next morning." She shuddered gently at the memory.

"Those poor things," Grammie said. "That's the kind of stuff that sticks with you for a lifetime." Her compassion went a long way toward softening Kitty's attitude. "What I can't understand is how no one missed her overnight. Or saw her lying there. Why was she screwing around on a roof in the dark anyway?"

"Single woman who lives alone, there's no one at home to miss her, and it gets dark early this time of year. Just last week, I came to work in the dark and went home the same way."

"But you never saw her ghost? Never attempted to help?" So much for the momentary truce between my mother and grandmother.

Mom sighed. "Do you really think so little of me?"

"I'm sorry, Kitty," Grammie muttered. "That wasn't fair." To bolster the apology, she reached out for her daughter-in-law's hand and gave it a squeeze.

"Apology accepted. Lily lived a reclusive life, but she did come and borrow books from time to time. I hadn't seen her for at least a few months before she passed and not at all since. I would have helped her if I had, and now that I know she didn't cross over, it explains a few minor mysteries that happen around this time of year."

"Such as," I prodded.

Her fingers twitched, so she busied them with scanning books back into the library system while she framed her response.

"I thought it was Martha and her bossy posse if you want to know the truth, but given this new information, I think Lily is the one with very particular ideas about outdoor holiday decor."

When that comment got a pair of mystified looks, she elaborated. "Haven't you noticed there's never a single live wreath left out long enough to turn orange in this entire town? You won't because they disappear first."

I couldn't say I had. "Someone took down one of the lighted garlands near the Nativity scene the other day, too."

"I thought the wreath police was Martha's doing, but now, I'm not so sure. Last year, Barb Dexter complained that someone had rearranged all her decorations. Or not complaining so much because she said the place looked a lot better afterward, but it wasn't her doing."

"Makes sense, I guess. Lily Evergreen lived on a Christmas tree farm. Seems like she might hold strong opinions on seasonal decorating."

"There's something else. One time, I missed a bauble when taking down the tree. It was one of those pretty little birds, Sadie. The ones you used to have and passed on to us. Anyway, after we put the tree out for pickup, I found that bird and several strands of tinsel in our mailbox. Half the town has a similar story. I've heard many of them over the past few years, but I never once suspected a ghost might be behind it all. They call her the Christmas Elf."

Grammie Dupree caught my eye. We exchanged a

telling glance before she turned her attention back to Kitty. "Can I assume we're going on a ghost hunt?"

Kitty shook her head slowly. "I can't go right now because I'm working," she replied. "And it seems like Lily's more active at night. All the stories I've ever heard start out with something like, you'll never guess what I found this morning."

From experience, though not my own, because I hadn't managed to muster up enough energy to affect anything in the physical world, I knew it wasn't easy for ghosts to move things around.

"Sounds like she's active in short bursts, doing small things before she runs out of gusto," I mused. "The key will be figuring out where she'll go next and getting there before she uses too much energy, burns out, and fades away. Looks like we're in for a round of the ghost version of Whackamole."

"Tell me more about Lily's death," Grammie leaned an elbow on the tall counter and tapped her fingers on the polished wood. "My belly's telling me that's one of the keys. Did they do an autopsy?"

"I don't know. You'd have to ask her family, but I doubt it. It looked like an accident, so why would they? I don't think there was any mystery about the cause of death. She fell, and when she couldn't get help, she succumbed to the elements."

"I s'pose not," Grammie replied. "Still don't think a star's worth dying for."

Mom shrugged. "Maybe Lily was searching for something—a sense of hope, a moment of peace, a way to feel closer to God. Whatever it was, she found her end in that Nativity display." She paused, looking off into the distance. "It's a tragic story."

"That makes two of those when it comes to Lily, and I can't help wondering why, if her death was an accident, she's still here. What was her unfinished business, and did it have anything to do with Abigail?"

"We need more information," Grammie banged a fist on the counter. "I don't suppose you know where Abigail's family moved?"

"I don't." Mom's lips formed a firm line. "And I wouldn't condone dredging up the painful past for them if I did."

"Lily's family, then. Can we set up something with this Chris?"

"It's Friday, but since I'm not exactly myself right now, we didn't plan a night out."

A short silence fell between the three of us, which Grammie broke by saying, "If this were one of my stories, we'd find someone to crack their computer so we could look at the police files. Maybe there's something in them that could shine a new light."

"You mean hack, not crack." But she'd given me an idea. "Still, that's an idea I might be able to work with."

Mom's eyebrows shot up, but her lids were narrowed. The perfect expression of both surprise and disapproval. "You know how to hack a computer? That's illegal."

I waved a hand to dismiss the accusation. "No, I don't, but I know Ernie, and whether he wants to admit it or not, he owes me at least one favor. I've solved a few cases for him."

Her expression softening, Mom gave me half a smile. "I'm sure he'll be thrilled to help, then." There was laughter in her tone to accompany the smile.

"He will not. He'll be ticked off and annoyed, but when isn't he? At least when it comes to me. Still, I think I can get him to let me look at whatever they have on file."

"Let's go." Grammie's feet ate up the floor on her way to the door. "We'll keep you posted, Kitty." I had no choice but to go with her when the invisible tether between me and my body snapped taut. I didn't want to be fully dead, but it would have been nice not to be yanked along willy-nilly whether I wanted to go or not.

"Be sure that you do," followed us out the door.

"When we get to the station, don't forget to keep a lid on your temper. Ernie and I have a unique relationship, and I'd like to keep that intact once things get back to normal. It's probably best to keep your cool with Carole Ann, too."

"I know how to handle people."

So did I, so I wasn't stupid enough to argue the point. "Whatever Carole Ann says, just ask if Ernie's around. It annoys her more if she can't get a rise out of you."

"I figured that out the last time." Grammie nodded. "I've dealt with that kind before."

"Ernie's got some bark and some bite, but he's a good man and a good cop. He didn't hesitate to lock up his own sister when she killed my former boss and then tried to kill me. We have a history, and it's been painful on both sides at times, so keep all of that in mind."

We'd pulled up and parked next to Ernie's cruiser, so I knew he'd be inside.

"You just tell me what to say, and I'll do my best to keep my face from saying anything else. Will that do it?"

"It will." And with our approach settled, we headed inside.

"Who did you kill this time??" Carole Ann had changed her hair. Not just the style but the color as well. I wasn't sure if I should be annoyed or flattered that she'd gone with something quite similar to mine.

"No one's dead. Is Ernie here?"

Her eyes trained on Grammie's face, Carole Ann picked up the phone and told Ernie I was there. I didn't hear his answer, but without dropping her gaze or blinking, Carole Ann pushed the button to unlock the door leading to the cells.

Despite my coaching, Grammie couldn't help herself. "Hope your face doesn't freeze like that."

She got an eye roll.

"Or maybe I hope it does." Grammie sailed through the door.

"Didn't I say not to let her goad you?"

I got no reply. We found Ernie in the records room, which boded well for our visit.

"No one's dead," Grammie kicked right in before I could coach her.

"Glad to hear it." Ernie didn't smile, but he wasn't scowling, either. "What can I do for you, Dupree?"

It took some talking, some patience, and a promise that I would try to butt out of any future investigations, which we both knew was as empty as Carole Ann's head. Still, Ernie hovered over Grammie's shoulder as she scanned both files.

"Son of a biscuit," she said when she'd laid one photo of each body on the table side-by-side. "Would you look at that?"

Ernie's language turned the air blue.

"How the hell did you know? Do you have any idea what this means?"

We gazed at the photos of two bodies found years apart, one a victim of murder, one a death of natural causes. Both were lying on their backs, hair splayed around white faces turned slightly to the left. Both left hands rested, palm up, beside their faces, and both right hands had been positioned over their hearts. Coincidence? I thought not.

"I do," Grammie said. "It means Lily Evergreen was murdered by the same person who murdered Abigail."

"No wonder she didn't cross over," I said while Ernie rubbed a hand over his forehead. A gesture I'd seen him make more than once in my presence. Probably because of it.

"How did you know," he repeated, turning to grasp her shoulders and give them a shake. "If you hadn't put those photos side by side....how did you know?"

"Doesn't matter. What matters is that if Abigail's killer is still in prison, who did this? Was it a copycat? Or was the wrong person convicted of a crime all those years ago?"

"I should have never let you in here. Now, I have a headache, both literally and figuratively."

"I'm sorry for that," Grammie said, and even I could tell she meant it. "It wasn't my plan to stir up trouble for you. I just wanted to know more about Lily Evergreen; it seemed like Abigail's death was the place to start. We...I wasn't expecting this, though."

Grabbing the rest of the photos, Ernie began to line them up. The similarities between both sets of posed limbs were chillingly unmistakable.

"What happens next?"

"These are closed cases. Can't reopen without new evidence, and I'm not sure this is enough to take to the judge. I'll look into it best I can. See what I see, then decide what to do. You'll be staying out of it."

"Sure."

He didn't look like he put much stock in her agreement, and it didn't help that she grabbed up one of the sheets of notes about Lily's death and glanced over it before he could yank it out of her hand.

"You promised."

"I promised to try, and I will."

"We won't get anything more from him," I told her. "Not yet, anyway. He'll have to cool off first, so we might as well go."

Nodding, she turned to leave, and when Ernie repeated his order to mind her own business, she gave him an over-the-shoulder wave and let his muttered cussing usher her out the door.

"I guess we opened a fine kettle of fish."

I didn't even correct her butchered idiom because she was right. We'd opened something, and now, it was time to figure out what and why. We needed to talk to Lily.

Chapter 24

Through the quiet night, I followed my grandmother from my house to the town's square. The silence between her footsteps settled around me like a ghostly embrace. As we neared the nativity scene, a lone figure stood in ethereal stillness. Short, dark curls framed a delicate face pale with death, but I could tell she'd also been pale in life. She wore jeans and an oversized flannel shirt, the fabric billowing gently in a phantom wind.

"Be easy," I muttered to my grandmother. "We don't want to scare her away."

When the ghost only smiled as she noted our presence, we cautiously continued, stopping when we were a few feet from her. I peered into her large blue eyes, searching for answers while she stood under scrutiny, showing no sign of fear. More, I could feel something emanating from her – a warmth that filled the chilled air like a sweet fragrance.

Finally, she spoke. Her voice was soft, melodic, and soothing. "You're Everly Dupree." She pointed to me. Ghost me. Not my body. "I've been waiting to meet you," she said. "I'm Lily Evergreen, and I need your help."

"Nice to meet you. I also need your help, but we can talk about that later. First, I'd like to ask you a few questions about Abigail's death because I don't think her boyfriend killed her. Do you?"

Lily slowly shook her head. "I never did."

The light finally dawned. "That's why you lived such a reclusive life. You knew her killer was still out there and thought he might come for you. And you know who it was, don't you?"

This time, Lily nodded.

"Can you tell me?"

Another head shake dashed my hopes that she would just be able to tell me since we were both on the same side of the veil.

"You can't because he murdered you, too,"

Lily's eyes widened, but she shook her head sadly. "No. Not exactly," she said her voice barely above a whisper.

"What do you mean by that?" Grammie's voice sounded extraordinarily loud when it broke through the hushed night.

"I've said all I can. Tell me how I can help you."

We did, and when we finished, we pressed her for more information she couldn't or wouldn't give. "Find the donkey, and all will be clear." Lily faded before I could say a word to stop her.

"Did you have to yell at her like that? You scared her away."

"Never mind that," Grammie flapped a hand at me. "Did you hear what she said? She wasn't murdered."

"Yeah, I heard it." I wanted to stomp my feet and do the walk of grump all the way back home, but it wasn't nearly as satisfying when stomping didn't make a sound. "Now what? Find the donkey? It's been missing for a week, and no one has seen wooden hide or hair of it. How does that help us?"

Ignoring my foul mood, Grammie shivered in the cold. "I guess we'll find out when we find it."

"That's not happening tonight, and you're cold. Let's get you home and into a warm bed. Tomorrow will be a busy day. We have to deal with the lighting contest and Martha, so we'll take a break from murder mysteries and enjoy what we can of the day."

This year's lighting contest would outshine last year's by a mile, or so Martha informed us when we arrived. She had no idea she'd made a pun, and the air around her still seemed colder than the seasonal chill. Still, even if she hadn't forgiven me, she needed my help, so she kept a civil tongue when we met to go over our notes. We'd left ourselves an hour to walk through the setup together and make any last-minute changes before the kick-off at seven.

"Snow sculptures first?" Martha didn't plan to take no for an answer, so we headed toward the mostly empty parking lot behind Curated Collections. "I don't know what we'd have done if we hadn't had that storm a couple of days ago."

"Hauled it in from Mackinaw, I reckon," Grammie said before I could feed her an answer. The gist was correct, even if the tone wasn't as respectful as Martha would like.

"Next year, I think we should try for a professional-level event. Did you know there's a whole snow-sculpting community out there? We could get television coverage. Wouldn't that be something? Really put Mooselick River on the map."

"Don't," I warned when Grammie opened her mouth to deliver what I assumed would be a snarky comment. Then, I grinned at her when she cocked an eyebrow at me because she knew the same observation had sprung to my mind. We were more alike than I remembered, even if she'd lost most of her filters.

When what had been six mounds of snow came into view, Grammie sucked in a breath. I would have done the same if I could. Banks of rented job lights turned night almost to day while teams of artists with all manner of interesting tools swarmed over five partially-constructed creations. Even at the amateur level, these sculptors meant business.

"How long have they been working?" Martha found Chris Evergreen standing nearby, his arms crossed, watching the activity with great interest. He'd offered to supervise the snow dumping and placement, so I didn't have to. Plus, as the husband of one of my closest friends, he knew all about my current situation, and this was his way of taking some of the pressure off me. The fact that Chris owned a Christmas tree farm and this was his busiest season only made the gesture more heart-warming.

"Sculpting began at dawn, but some of these guys have been here all week. They wanted to be sure we piled the snow properly. I guess there's a right way and a wrong way."

When I picked out one figure wearing a dark hoodie under his jacket, I figured that explained the mystery man I'd seen around town a few times. Since It looked like Chris had things well in hand, I blessed him silently, and we moved on to the town square to check on the tents and heaters set up as warming stations.

Most of the vendors had arrived and were setting up to do a brisk business for the evening. The weather was perfect, and even the judges' station looked festive with bows at the corners of the table and a pretty evergreen swag draped across the front. Lighted, of course, to fit in with the day's theme.

"Everything looks good." Grammie offered a rare compliment that loosened up the last of the ice in Martha's attitude. "You've done a great job here."

"We have," Martha agreed. "We're getting good at throwing these events."

With that, Martha proved her forgiveness by pulling a thermos of hot chocolate from her bag and offering me a cup.

"We did go slightly over budget because Chris insisted on renting those lights so the sculptors could keep working once it got dark. I think that will encourage people to return tomorrow for the judging. It was an inspired idea." Martha gave credit where it was due, then moved on to check things in the town square.

The Nativity scene looked a bit odd from its recent losses, but you had to give small-town people credit for being helpful. Or for being intentionally amusing while being helpful. The empty spaces left by the missing farm animals had been mysteriously filled. One with a large, lighted reindeer lawn ornament and the other with one of those realistic deer-shaped shooting targets made from high-impact foam. And just for fun, several tree ornaments hung from the antlers.

I also spotted a few other additions that Martha hadn't approved. Ranged near the empty manger were half a dozen garden gnomes, one in the form of Darth Vader, another wearing biker's leathers and flipping the bird. Tucked among the remaining farm animals, I counted six more plastic flamingos, two stuffed bears, and a giant rooster made of pressed metal.

Martha took one look and wigged while Grammie Dupree bit her lips hard enough to draw blood and still couldn't stop a fit of giggles.

"It's blasphemy. How can you find this funny? I'm positively outraged."

Martha idled at *outraged,* so that wasn't anything new.

"I'm sorry," Grammie wheezed. "But that's funny. No matter how you look at it."

When Martha merely glared, she sobered up enough to offer to help hide the worst offenses before anyone else showed up. "But I think we should leave the deer. Just maybe take off the ornaments. What do you think?"

"Whatever." Martha's cold indifference had returned. "I think we should split up and meet back here in half an hour." So saying, she sailed off with her stiff posture telling me exactly how she felt.

"What crawled up her butt?"

"Nothing the doesn't already live there anyway."

The half-hour passed uneventfully, but the time apart hadn't dented Martha's attitude, so Grammie and I steered clear of her until it was time to round up the judges. While they did, I wandered as far from them as my tether would allow, my gaze moving from one happy face to the next, ensuring the event proceeded smoothly.

Once or twice, I forgot myself enough to say hello to someone but felt completely out of place. I probably should have tagged along to make sure Grammie Dupree kept herself in line, but I needed a break, so I kept moving, taking in the lively scenes before me.

The chatter of people enjoying the festivities filled the air along with, I assumed, the scent of frying dough. I preferred mine with a generous layer of melted butter, cinnamon, and a thick dusting of powdered sugar. Remembering the aromas and flavors did nothing to improve my mood.

Everywhere I looked, I saw families, young people, and elderly couples, all drawn to the beauty of the lights and the promise of shared joy that the season brings.

With temps in the chill zone, festival goers lined up at the coffee and hot chocolate booths as well as the heating stations positioned at intervals on either side of the street. Despite the cold, the crowd remained festive, as things should be at Christmastime.

Satisfied, I headed toward the petting zoo.

"Piggy!" Jamie Anderson's squeal of joy blended with the noises coming from the fenced-in area where five adorable piglets scrambled and played. A sixth piglet had abandoned his siblings in favor of hovering near the pen door.

"Pet piggy." Jamie tugged on his mother's coat. "Please."

"We're in line to pet the pigs already, honey. We just have to wait our turn."

"No. This piggy," Jamie insisted, pointing toward the quivering piglet.

"Those piglets aren't part of the petting zoo, honey. I think they're just here to be close to their mama if they need her. We can watch them play, but we mustn't touch."

But when Jane's attention turned away, Jamie's quick fingers arrowed toward the latch on the piglet's pen.

The world, at least the living world, slowed down to a crawl as I watched events unfold, but was unable to do a thing to stop them.

"Don't touch that," I yelled into the tinny echo that was my new reality while Jamie Anderson fiddled with the latch. What a waste of energy. He didn't hear me, nor did his mother when I got in her face. Nimble-fingered and blessed with a double dose of curiosity, the boy could make trouble from nothing at all.

He looked right at me and smiled when he flipped the lever to set the wriggling piglet free. A blur of pink flashed past me, weaving in and around the feet of those waiting in line.

"Hey!" Shouts went up, but that only seemed to spur the tiny beast on as he dodged and spun to avoid the hands that wanted to return him to safety. "Catch him."

"Over here."

The piglet bulleted through a knot of bystanders as if he were a bowling ball scattering human pins in his wake. He dodged left, right, and left again so quickly it was impossible to predict where he might go next.

Quicker on his feet than he looked, Tim Bennett dived as the little beast raced past but ended up with wet pants and a fistful of slush for his efforts.

"Cut him off," I yelled to be heard over the pig's shrill

squeals. Didn't matter since no one was listening to me, anyway.

Seeing a slim chance of escape, the piglet turned on a dime and headed for the narrow alley between two buildings. If he made it through to the parking area behind, the odds of catching him dropped to nearly zero. Speaking of zero, with projected overnight temperatures nearing that number, the silly pig's life depended on someone stopping him.

I didn't think about how to get to the mouth of the alley. I just shifted and was there with the line between me and my body pulled tight.

"Boo." I leaned down and waved my arms at the pig, who put on the brakes. Yes, animals can see ghosts, or as Grammie Dupree called me, disembodied spirits. The pig's eyes filled with fear as his tiny hooves slipped and skidded across packed snow. He managed to turn himself around, his feet scrabbling for purchase.

I thought I had him then.

"What's going on?" Grammie Dupree stepped out of the shadows just in time to scare the little pig half out of his skin. Turning, he buzzed right past me and headed for the snow sculptures again.

"Fan out." Patrea, Chris, Neena, David, Jacy, and Brian had been watching the sculptures slowly take shape while my parents had followed Grammie when she'd come to find me. Between all of us, we could surely catch one tiny piglet, right?

Wrong.

The bundle of pink and nerves arrowed for the untouched sixth pile of snow, stopped, and looked back at me.

"He can see me," I shouldn't have been surprised. Molly hadn't been fooled by the grandmotherly body snatch, either.

He could have run. The silly animal had enough of a lead on us to get right away, but that wasn't his goal. Instead, he went to digging in the pile of snow, just as fast as his little hooves would move, and managed to make a decent hole before Brian reached down and grabbed him.

"Everly, look," Grammie hissed and drew my attention to where Lily stood near the pile of snow. "I think she had something to do with calling that piglet here. We should keep digging."

Since my instincts were singing the same song, I didn't argue the point, but I did do the math.

"Ask Chris how many sculptors were supposed to be here. I thought we only had five on the list. Why are there six piles of snow?"

When she relayed the question, he shrugged. "I figured we had a late entry, maybe a team of kids since this pile is small, and that someone else supervised the drop on this one."

"I don't think so. Martha would have alerted the presses if she'd agreed to a youth entry."

Once Brian had returned the piglet to its pen, he rejoined us and took up one of the shovels we'd borrowed from the sculptors. With four men digging, it didn't take long to unearth Clyde and then Bessie.

"How did that pig know these were here?" Jacy said.

"Some pigs sniff out truffles. Maybe this one sniffs out wooden farm animals," Patrea said.

"It had a little help." At my nod, Grammie told the

others about Lily. When the news flummoxed Chris, Patrea took his hand and gave it a squeeze.

"Is she still here?" He looked around. "Tell her she's missed." He'd gone a bit pale around the edges but helped release the cow and donkey from their icy prison and carry them into the light. Lily drifted back from wherever she'd been hiding just long enough to run a hand over the donkey's head, give Chris a sad smile he couldn't see, and then she was gone again.

"Nothing seems to be broken, but I'll have Martha let me repaint them over the summer." The expert when it came to wood, my dad checked things over. "What's this?" his brow knit when his questing fingers found a hole. "I think there's something in here. Help me tip him over." That last was for Drew and the rest of the men.

A closer look revealed a deep knothole on the inside of the donkey's hind leg, and when they got him flipped over into the right angle, we all heard a rattling sound and saw something fall out.

"Don't touch it," I yelled, and my mother repeated as my father reached down. "It could have fingerprints."

"I've got it." Given his training, Drew carried a small multi-tool in his pocket. He flicked open the pliers and used the jaws to gently lift the object up and into the light where we could all see it better.

"What is it?" Jacy glanced up, confusion written all over her face.

"That's a pipe stem," Grammie said with finality. "Vulcanite. Hasn't aged well, but what do you expect when it's been stuck in a donkey's leg for years?" Leaning over, she put her hand on Drew's and gently turned it so she could get a better look. "Some toothmarks, but not much evidence of nicotine staining."

"It must have been her killer's. I think it fell off during the struggle or something, and she found it and dropped it into that knothole to leave a clue, but no one found it, and then they stopped using the Nativity scene, so it sat there all this time."

Jacy tapped her fingers on the donkey's back. "Okay, but why bury it out here? Assuming the killer knew it was in there, why wouldn't he just destroy it."

"Because he didn't," Grammie and I spoke at the same time, but only one of us was heard. Except for by my mother, of course, who caught on to our line of thinking right away.

"Lily hid the stem and then buried these animals here to bring our attention to the evidence," she said.

"Worked, didn't it?" Grammie almost chortled.

But then, Chris popped her bubble. "Not if we don't know who it belongs to."

"Even then, I don't think this will be enough to reopen the case." As an attorney, Patrea had a better handle on the finer points of the law than the rest of us. "Not if her death was ruled accidental, anyway."

"Okay. What do we do now?"

Chapter 25

"First thing," Neena finally found he voice, "is to get these animals under cover before we draw a crowd." Already, we'd pulled the focus of some of the people who'd drifted in to watch the sculpting.

"And in another half hour, I'll have to be in place to introduce the lighting contest judges, so we'll need to be quick about it, too," Grammie said.

"We can do quick," Drew grabbed one end of the donkey and motioned for David to take the other. Brian and Chris followed their lead while my father went on ahead to hold the door for them since they'd decided to hide the animals in the back room of Curated Collections. No one would look for them there.

Falling behind the crowd, I stayed within the bounds of my tether while questions surrounding Lily's death spiraled through my head. First, if the same person killed both friends, why had he waited more than thirty years to go after Lily? Had she discovered something after all that time that led her to believe the police had arrested the wrong person? Had the real killer left town after the first murder and then returned? Or was this a copycat thing? All good questions with no way for me to get the answers until I talked to Lily.

"Lily!" I yelled loud enough to make Grammie and my mother flinch. "Are you here? We need to talk." If anyone had answers, it was her. "Lily! I know you're around."

Around, but not willing or perhaps able to help. Fine. I'd solve this without her.

The timeline didn't make sense. Lily's body had to have been repositioned after her death, meaning she had to have hidden the pipe stem while she was alive and the killer was nearby.

What had happened that day, and why? The questions asked in every mystery since the beginning of time.

According to what I'd seen of the police reports, no one had questioned Lily's death being anything other than an accident. Closing my eyes, I pictured the scene as Ernie had described it. The stable stood roughly where it was now, and he'd found a stepladder at the back with one set of footprints in the snow that dusted the roof. There'd been a mark where she'd laid the star down as she prepared to secure it to the post and footprints right at the tallest edge of the slanted roof.

Anyone looking at the evidence would have come to the same conclusion: Lily had gone up there in the dark, had not realized how close she was to the edge, and had fallen. The report noted injuries consistent with the short drop. She had a broken ankle on her left side, a broken wrist on her right, and a minor bump on the head. Injuries that on their own were not life-threatening.

Had anyone come by, they'd have heard Lily yelling for help. No one had. Or no one with good intentions, anyway.

In my mind's eye, the scene played out. Lily hurt,

209

helpless on the ground, and getting colder by the minute as she crawled into the stable where she'd probably intended to use bales of hay and straw for insulation. At the very least, she'd get in out of the wind.

When the shadowy figure appeared, Lily must have felt such relief. She'd been found. She was safe. Except she wasn't.

Did he tell her why before he left her there to die? Did he wait and watch while she shivered and quaked? And then wait longer until she stopped? How long did it take for her to succumb? When had she found the pipe stem?

With all these questions rolling around in my head, I decided it was time to put myself in Lily's position. Literally. While the others continued to discuss what to do next, I lowered my astral body to the floor. Using only my left leg and right arm, I crawled a few inches. It was awkward and difficult, but it gave me a good idea of Lily's body position as she made her way into the stable.

As I neared the donkey, I saw the knothole clearly. It wouldn't have taken more than a few seconds to reach around and drop the pipe stem inside. Since she was standing over me, watching my actions, I asked my mother if she could see my hand as I mimed the action I thought Lily had taken.

She shook her head, no, and I rose.

"This is what I think happened," I had her parrot my words for the others to hear. "Lily was on the roof of the stable. She'd attached the star and was probably adjusting it or admiring her handiwork when she got too close to the edge and fell. There's no evidence anyone was up there with her."

Grammie nodded. "That's right. We saw the police

report."

"She crawled into the stable, presumably to take shelter while she waited for help. There was a bump on her head, which was consistent with the fall. I saw that noted on the report as well, but we all know there was nothing natural about this death."

Nods of agreement and one or two suggestions came my way, but I couldn't get rid of the movie playing in my head and needed to talk it all the way through.

"At this point, or maybe before, our suspect arrives and sees that Lily is hurt. They talk. Maybe he even tries to help, but then he says something that lets her know he was the one who killed Abigail. She reacts, and now, he knows the only way to keep his secret is if Lily dies."

Mom took up the next part proving we did think alike at times. "Lily's already done half the work for him by taking a tumble, so all he really has to do is make sure no one sees her, and she can't call out for help."

"According to the police report, temps were in the single digits that night," Grammie was also catching on to my thinking. "If the fall knocked the wind out of her, she'd have laid on the ground for a long enough that her body heat would melt snow and get her clothes wet."

"Hypothermia can occur in as little as five minutes," Drew knew his survival facts. "If she wasn't moving. She could hold out a little longer if she used motion to generate more body heat. She could have made it through the night if she'd burrowed into the hay."

Drew wasn't the only one because David had the medical experience to back up his theory. "It had to have happened fast. Probably not as fast as five minutes, but not longer than ten or fifteen. A cold-hearted snake could stand there and promise to help her, hold out hope until she passed out, then walk away without getting his hands dirty."

"So we're looking for a cold-hearted asshole who smokes a pipe and has the patience to bide his time." I'd bet that Dad's hair had gone poofy under his hat, considering he didn't even bat an eyelash when my mother chided him for his language. He hit the nail on the head, though.

"Sounds about right," David looked at the faces around him. "Do we know of anyone who fits the bill?"

I had Grammie tell them about the hoodie-wearing guy, but he was the only one who came to mind, and I hadn't the first clue what he looked like.

"The town's full of strangers, we've got a lighting contest to finish, and no idea where to start looking. Why don't we leave Clyde and Bessie where they are and get back out there? It's probably best to split up and pair up to cover more ground. Meet back at the Nativity in half an hour to compare notes."

Splitting up made sense, as did pairing up for safety. With everyone else naturally paired up, that left me with Grammie, and since it was almost time for her to introduce the judges, we made our way toward the gazebo, where she'd make the announcement.

"There you are," Martha bustled over, her face a mask of disapproval. "Another minute, and you'd be late."

"Another minute, and I'd still be five minutes early," Grammie muttered and didn't do me any favors with Martha, but she wasn't wrong about the time.

While we waited for our cue, I watched the crowd. Somewhere in that sea of faces might lurk the smile of a murderer. It was enough to give chills to a dead person. Or an almost-dead person.

With a little coaching, Grammie did a bang-up job of the introductions, and while the judges set off to do their thing, I caught sight of that hunched-over, hoodie-wearing figure I'd seen several times.

"Let's go," I said, pointing to where he'd gone, "That way."

That way was, of course, the opposite direction from where most people were heading, so it felt a little like a fish swimming upstream to get past the throng. When we did, we found ourselves closer to the outskirts of the action, where fewer lights cut through the darkness and not all that far from where I'd found Amber Hale's body the year before. I shuddered at the memory, but it was my grandmother who jumped half out of her skin when a hand landed on her shoulder.

"Everly, isn't it?" Scott Vestry's face broke into a genuine smile. "I have to say, you and Martha know how to throw a party. I haven't had this much fun in boring old Mooselick River since ...never, actually. I've never had this much fun here. It's why I don't come back to visit more than once every five or ten years."

"Thanks." We'd lost track of our quarry, so while Grammie kept talking, I moved past Scott to scan the area but came up empty. "We do our best to make things nice."

"Lost him," I told her, not that she couldn't see that for herself. She shrugged and turned back toward the center of town, with Scott following. If nothing else, she wouldn't be on her own if we did run into the guy.

As we passed the front of the Nativity scene, Scott

laughed. "Garden gnomes and flamingos. I don't recall seeing those in the story before."

"Kids," Grammie said and shrugged. "Martha wasn't amused, but in her case, I think that's a terminal condition."

A second laugh rolled out of him, but I sensed no malice in it. Or in him. My mistake.

"I almost wish we hadn't pulled this old thing out of mothballs," Grammie told him as she plunked down on a bale of hay to rest her feet for a minute. "It's brought back a lot of memories for people, and not all of them good."

"Can you blame them? The memory of Lily's body sprawled across the hay is one I'll never forget."

Standing behind him and off to his left, I had a perfect view when Grammie's gaze shot up, and her eyes fixed on his pocket. The pocket where I remembered, he carried a pipe. All the pieces fell into place just about the time I realized we might be in danger.

"You're wondering how I came by that memory, aren't you?" All the hearty good cheer had left his voice.

"No, I think I know exactly how that came about. Why'd you kill her?"

He took half a step, and she rose to her feet. Good. That was good. She stood in a better position to defend herself.

"What do you mean? I didn't kill Lily."

"I meant Abigail," Grammie's voice went hard. I circled around to get a look at Scott's face. With the judging imminent, most of the crowd had migrated toward the other end of town, leaving us virtually alone here until someone else from our group showed up. It wouldn't be much longer since our half-hour was just about up.

"I'm not a mean person," Scott pulled out his pipe and bit down on the stem while he tried to defend himself from my scowling grandmother.

"Quit giving him the dirty looks. You need to humor him to keep him talking." The look she flashed me wasn't complimentary, but she did wipe the wrinkles off her forehead.

"No, I can see you're not," she said, getting on with the program. "You helped us with all of this."

The pipe went back into his pocket.

"I just wanted to help Abby see, but she didn't want to."

"See what?"

"What was good for her? I was good for her." Rage ate the affability from his features a bite at a time, leaving no trace behind. "She didn't see me. No one ever sees me." He'd flipped fully to the dark side, and Grammie was in trouble. Her gaze flicked to mine as he took a second step toward her.

"You don't want to hurt me," she said. "I can see what Abby didn't." She bought herself a few seconds, but it wouldn't be enough. "I see you, Scott."

He took two more steps as panic replaced her carefully blank expression, then stopped when the ghost of Lily rose between him and the woman he wanted to hurt.

"No." Scott shook his head and took one short step back. "You can't be here. I let you die."

"Same as killing in my book," Grammie dumped a little gas on the fire.

"Shut up," he took one more step and backhanded her. Shrinking from him, she tipped her face down, but angry color flared across her cheek, and I didn't even think twice; I dived for my body.

"Make room." In the heat of the moment, I didn't think about how or why, just that the best way to protect her was to protect myself, and I needed my body for that, so I took it over. Just in time for Lily to say something else, I couldn't hear over the adrenaline-fueled energy buzzing through my limbs. It felt good to be real again. Or real-ish, I supposed.

When Scott stepped through her, Lily went to smoke and reformed several feet away, but I only caught the motion out of the corner of my eye because, at that moment, I had better things to do. Like dance back to avoid another vicious swipe.

"You missed," I taunted. Or Grammie did. I couldn't be sure.

His next swing also went wide, and the fury had him turning an open hand into a fist. Things were about to get real. He came at me again, the blow glancing off my right shoulder instead of my face, but it was enough to make my arm half numb. Good thing I'd worked on my left jab because I got one, and while he shook it off, I ducked under his arm to get some distance.

That was my mistake because I went the wrong way and ended up trapped between him and a stack of hay bales. Triumph slid over his face, only marred slightly by the bleeding lip I'd just given him.

Knowing he had me, Scott moved into a crouch and got ready to take me down. I shrieked, finally, and heard answering shouts coming from outside. Help was coming.

Unfortunately, Scott realized help was coming, too, and instead of giving up, decided to take me down before they arrived. I saw my death in his eyes right as he sprang.

Several things happened at once. Lily rose up behind him with a garden gnome clutched in one ghostly hand and took aim just as a figure in a dark hoodie launched from outside and knocked Scott into the statue of Joseph, who banged into one of the wise men. All three went down like dominoes, with Scott and his assailant at the bottom of the pile. The garden gnome whizzed past my head.

"Sorry," Lily looked at me with no small amount of humor, then turned to smoke as my friends and family converged. Drew went for me while Chris helped my savior to his feet, and David and my dad took control of Scott.

With the distraction of everyone talking at once, I let go of my hold on my body and popped out of it just in time to see Patrea staring at the man who'd saved me. Eyes wide and glistening with unshed tears, her expression carried a mix of shock and happiness.

"Justin? Is that really you?"

"Hi, sis." Shocked, Patrea stared at the man who'd grown from the boy who'd run from his family so many years before. "Sorry, I missed the wedding."

While the siblings went outside to reconnect, Jacy and Neena ran to get Ernie, who took Scott into custody and ordered us to come to the police station to give our statements as soon as the lighting contest was over.

I was glad he'd given us the extra time. With the

mystery of her death solved, Lily wouldn't want to stick around long. She'd earned her rest, and I wanted to give it to her.

"It's time," Grammie said. "Are you ready, Lily?"

"Say your goodbyes," Lily said, her body beginning to fade. She'd used a lot of energy during the confrontation, and when her features blurred, I knew she was down to the last of her reserves.

"Grammie," my voice barely rose above a whisper. "I'm not ready to lose you again."

Her mouth curved into a soft smile. "I'll always be with you, my darling. And with you, my son." She turned to my father, laid her hand along his cheek, and pulled his face close to rest her forehead against his. Whatever she whispered was for him alone and evoked a misty smile.

When she let him go, he turned away momentarily while she moved on to my mother and held out her arms. "I'm sorry, Kitty. You know I hate being wrong and, worse having to admit to it, but in your case, I was. Dead wrong. You're a good woman, and I should have seen that in you all along."

"There were mistakes made on both sides. I can wish we'd seen them sooner while still being thankful for this chance to put the past away. Go into the light now with my forgiveness and love, Sadie, and feel sure we'll see each other again."

They embraced, and then, it was time.

"Come." She moved close but waited for me to bridge the distance. "It's time for me to go into the light and give you back your body. Lily, are you ready?"

Lily nodded. "Hurry," she mouthed. She'd hung on

long enough for us to say our goodbyes, for which I owed her a debt of gratitude.

"I can't thank you enough for all you've done, Lily."

Lily smiled, and as she did, light rose to outline her body with liquid flame. "I can't stay."

"It's time," my grandmother repeated as she took Lily's hand in one of hers, then reached for mine with the other.

In the blur and rush of light and sound that followed, I only remember seeing my grandmother's face, her eyes filled with love for me, and her last words burned into my brain. "Don't be a damn fool. Marry that boy."

"Yes, Gramme. I will."

A thousand bees buzzed in my ears. Not this again, I thought as a curtain of darkness snuffed out the light. Again, I drifted through endless night until a sound penetrated the darkness.

"Everly. Wake up, honey. Come on. Open your eyes."

"Drew?" My voice sounded harsh, like the croaking bullfrogs that sang each night at camp. But the sound and feel of it anchored me in the security of knowing I was back in my body. Of feeling Drew's arms cradling me against his chest.

"It worked. She's back."

My eyelids felt like they scraped sand over glass when I opened them. "You're a sight for sore eyes."

He crushed me to him, squeezed the breath out of me, and I didn't mind one bit. He smelled of sweat and man and life. All things I would never take for granted again. My grandmother had given me a good piece of parting advice. One I didn't intend to ignore.

"I don't have a ring, and my knees are still too wobbly

for kneeling, but I refuse to wait one more minute. Drew Parker, you're the other half of my heart, the rock that gives me strength."

"The wind beneath your wings?" Neena's voice came from behind me.

"Shut up, and let her finish." I heard the tears in Jacy's voice. "This is a private moment."

"That they're having in front of everyone."

His face was so close to mine I couldn't miss the amused sparkle in Drew's eyes. "I come with an entourage, but if that's not a problem for you, I'm asking if you'll have me and if I can have you. Not just for today, but until I cross over into the light for real."

Jacy sniffled.

"I know it's my turn, and so I'm asking. Drew Parker, will you marry me?"

"Yes," he said, though his answer was muffled by hooting and cheers from our friends. "Of course, I will."

-The End-

Made in the USA
Monee, IL
14 September 2023

42738939R00132